AF439936

Murder at the River

AN EMMA WILSON MYSTERY BOOK 1

KYLA HARRIS

Chapter 1

June 17th

I unlocked the door to Emma's Haven, my bookstore located in downtown Athens, Georgia. The familiar bell jingled, signaling the start of another day. Warm rays of the rising sun shone through the large display windows, reflecting off the smooth wooden floors. As summer approached and most college students left for break, the town's pace slowed down, but my little store remained a sanctuary for avid readers in the area.

The interior of the store was lined with dark wooden shelves, packed to the brim with books of all shapes and sizes. Each shelf proudly displayed a small brass plaque, labeled with categories such as "Classics," "Mystery & Suspense," and "Local Authors." I took pride in the organization of my collection; every book had its designated spot, yet the shelves had just enough chaos to invite curiosity.

The center of the store was dominated by a massive, plush sofa covered in a colorful patchwork quilt. This was where my regulars often gathered, their conversations providing the background ambiance for my day. In front of it, a circular wooden coffee table exhibited partially completed puzzles and a stack of literary magazines.

On the left side of the sofa, a reading nook nestled in the corner, with a cushioned window seat that offered a picturesque view of the bustling streets of downtown. Sunlight was gently refracted by the stained-glass sun-catcher hanging from the ceiling, casting beautiful rainbow patterns around the store as the day progressed.

At the back of the store, there was a checkout counter made of sturdy oak. It had witnessed its fair share of history over the years. A row of unique coffee mugs sat on one end, each with its own story.

But today, something was off. As soon as I stepped inside, I could sense it. The sound of dripping water was the first thing I noticed. I thought it was just the rain outside, a drizzle tapping against the windows, but the sun was shining brightly.

I followed the sound to the back of the bookstore, where the bathroom was located. The moment I opened the door, my heart sank. The floor was a mess of puddles. Water was pouring from the wall near the toilet, creating a small stream that snaked its way across the tiles and out into the main room.

I felt a surge of panic and rushed to shut off the main water valve. I grabbed a mop and some towels, frantically trying to stem the flow of water, but it was clear this was more than I could handle. The books sitting on the shelves nearby were at risk; their covers were already beginning to curl from the moisture in the air.

My hand reached for my phone, and I quickly dialed Roy's number. He was a reliable plumber that I had worked with in the past. As the phone rang, I continued to push water toward the bathroom, trying my best to contain the mess.

"Morning, Emma," Roy answered. "What's up?"

"Roy, I need you here, like, yesterday. I've got a busted pipe in the bathroom, and my bookstore will soon turn into a swimming pool."

"Got it. I'll be there in twenty. Hang tight."

I hung up, took a deep breath, and texted John and Victoria, my employees on the morning shift. John had been working at the store for over two years, while Victoria was a second-year student at the University. She had started working here just six months ago.

First, I messaged John. **"Emergency at the bookstore,"** I typed quickly. **"Broken water pipe in the bathroom. Can you come ASAP?"**

Then I sent a similar message to Victoria. **"Store is flooded. Need you here now. Broken pipe in the bathroom. "**

After hitting the send button, I dialed my husband Daniel's number. It was summer break, so Daniel, a professor of biology at the University, was mostly working from home. He answered on the second ring with a cheerful tone. "Can't bear to be away from me already?"

"Hey, Dan," I said, trying to keep the frustration out of my voice. "We've got a problem at the bookstore. A pipe burst and now there's water all over the place. I already called Roy, but it's a mess."

Daniel's tone turned serious. "Oh no, that sounds like a disaster. Are you okay?"

"Yeah, I'm fine, just stressed out. The water damaged the wall and floor in the bathroom, and now it's beginning to seep into the main room."

"Do you want me to come over and help? I'm not doing much today."

I thought about it for a moment, picturing him traipsing through the water-soaked bathroom. "No, that's okay. Roy's should be here any minute, and I've got John and Victoria on the way. We'll manage. Could you pick up Oliver from daycare this afternoon? I might be here for a while, dealing with the water damage and all." Oliver was our adorable son.

"Yeah, of course. I'll go get Oliver from daycare. Just focus on getting everything sorted out at the bookstore." Daniel said. "Call me if you need anything else. Oh, and I was thinking about inviting Benjamin over for dinner. Is that okay with you?"

"Yeah, that's fine. I have to go now. Love you."

"Love you too," Daniel said before ending the call.

As if on cue, Roy burst through the door. "I'm here. What's the situation?"

"As you can see, we've got quite a mess on our hands." I led him to the bathroom.

Roy examined the damage with a knitted brow, his toolbox clanging as he set it on the floor. "Let's see what we're dealing with," he said, rolling up his sleeves.

I stepped back, giving him room to work.

"Seems like a broken pipe to me. I'll have to turn off the water, tear through the drywall, and replace the damaged section of the pipe. It shouldn't take too long," Roy said.

"I've already shut off the water," I reminded him. Roy got to work without another word.

Just then, the front door creaked open, and John and Victoria rushed into the store. Their eyes widened in shock as they surveyed the chaos.

"Emma!" John called out. "What happened?"

"A broken water pipe. Roy is here to fix it, but we need to start cleaning up this mess."

"Of course," Victoria said. "What do you want me to do, boss?"

"Grab buckets and mops from the storage room. Let's get rid of that big pool of water." I pointed in the direction of our modest supply area. "John, can you relocate those books nearest to the water to a drier spot?"

"Absolutely," John nodded as he and Victoria hurried off.

Mops in hands, Victoria and I set out to remove the water from the flooded area. The scent of dampness hung heavily in the air.

"I think we should prop open the door so that the water dries faster," Victoria suggested.

"That's an excellent idea," I said, making my way to the front and swinging the door open.

"I hope we can open on time today," Victoria muttered.

"We still have an hour and a half until 11 o'clock. That should be plenty of time for Roy to fix the pipe and for us to clean the floor," I reassured her.

"Unfortunately, the bathroom won't be available for customers today as we still need to repair the drywall," I added. "We'll have to put up a sign about it."

"I'll make a sign that says, 'No Bathroom'," John offered.

The sound of Roy tightening the last bolt brought a swell of relief to my chest. I watched as he wiped his brow, clearly satisfied with his work. "That should do it," he announced, straightening up.

"Thank you so much!" I gushed.

"Happy to help, Emma." Roy flashed me a warm smile. "Just make sure you keep an eye on the pipe for the next few days. If you see any leaks, give me a call right away."

"Sure," I said, giving him a firm handshake before he gathered his tools and left. Swiveling around to face John and Victoria, I said, "Okay, let's finish up the cleaning and get ready to open the store on time."

***

As I flipped the sign to 'Open,' the first of my regulars, Mrs. Harper, ambled in. Her presence was as reliable as the ticking of the antique clock on the wall. "Good morning, Emma!"

"Morning, Mrs. Harper," I replied, smoothing down my floral knee-length skirt. "It's good to see you. Any new adventures in the garden this week?"

"Oh, you know me, always trying to outsmart those squirrels. But I'm here to find a new mystery to dive into. Got anything new?"

I led her to a display of our latest arrivals, pointing out a novel with a particularly clever plot. "This one has been flying off the shelves. It's set in a small town much like ours."

Mrs. Harper clapped her hands in delight. "Perfect! I'll take it. And how about you, dear? Any plans for the summer?"

"Well, we've been thinking about taking a little road trip. Maybe head up to the mountains, find a quiet spot by a lake."

"That sounds wonderful. Sometimes, a little adventure is just what we need."

We exchanged a knowing glance as she headed toward the counter while I packaged her newly purchased book.

When I was busy rearranging the travel section in the afternoon, Alice breezed into the bookstore. Tall and fit, she moved with a confident grace that turned heads wherever she went. Her auburn hair was pulled back into a sleek ponytail, highlighting her striking features and piercing green eyes that seemed to take in everything at once.

Alice was a journalist through and through, always on the move, always looking for the next big story. Today, she wore a white sleeveless tank top and black trouser pants. She carried a large leather tote slung over her shoulder, filled with notebooks, pens, and her ever-present recorder.

"Emma, you're not going to believe who I'm interviewing today," she exclaimed. Before I could probe for details, she shifted gears. "Hey, why don't you come with me to Riverside Park for a swim tomorrow morning? It's supposed to be another scorcher, and the water will be divine."

I sighed. "I'd love to, Alice, but you won't believe the morning I've had. The water pipe burst overnight, and the bathroom was practically a swimming pool when I got here. I've just got it fixed, but the drywall is a wreck."

"Oh no, that's awful! Do you need help finding someone to fix the drywall?"

"I'll manage. Let's plan for a swim next week?"

"Deal! I'll hold you to that. You need a break, Emma." Alice glanced at her watch. "I've got to run, my interview is in twenty minutes and I can't be late. This one's a biggie."

Curiosity piqued, I asked, "Who is it?"

Her grin widened. "It's a secret for now, but let's just say it could be a huge scoop. I'll tell you all about it when I see you next. Wish me luck!"

With that, Alice hugged me quickly and dashed out the door. I watched her go, her presence always a whirlwind of excitement.

***

As the clock hit five o'clock, a wave of fatigue washed over me. The long day of organizing shelves, assisting customers, and trying to solve the water crisis had taken its toll. I stretched my limbs, feeling the aches in my muscles.

"Sophia, Evelyn," I called out to my afternoon shift employees, who were busy organizing the front display. The twins looked up in unison.

"I'm heading out. Could you two make sure everything's locked up tight when you close at seven?"

"Of course, boss," Sophia replied. Evelyn nodded, "We'll handle everything. Don't worry!"

I couldn't help but smile. Hiring the twins had been one of my better decisions. They were hardworking, and brought a cheerful atmosphere to the store, making even the busiest days feel more manageable.

"Remember to double-check the back door and the windows in the kids' section," I reminded them. "And the cash register, don't forget to log out."

"We've got it all under control," Evelyn assured me, waving a hand dismissively. They had closed up many times before, but my manager's instinct to double-check never faded.

"See you tomorrow," I said, heading for the door. They chorused a goodnight, their voices blended into a melody.

Chapter 2

The sun started its descent, casting elongated shadows over the manicured lawns of Pine Street. As I turned into the driveway, the sight of our home instantly put me at ease. The exterior of our house was painted a crisp white with dark green shutters to match the surrounding landscape. Colorful flower beds and a lush green lawn promised a relaxing stroll through the front yard.

I parked the car and walked toward the front porch. The swing and hanging baskets of petunias invited me to take a seat. The screen door let out a small creak as I stepped inside. The cool air of the interior greeted me, carrying the aroma of sizzling steaks and hints of garlic and pepper. Just as I was about to set down my purse, a little tornado came barreling toward me.

"Mommy!" Oliver crashed into my legs, his chubby arms wrapping around me in a fierce hug.

I scooped him up, burying my face in his soft, curly hair. "Hello, my little man," I murmured, peppering his cheek with kisses.

"Hey babe, you're home," Daniel appeared in the kitchen doorway, dish towel in hand. At 32 years old, he exuded a strength that came from physical fitness and quiet confidence. His sandy brown hair was tousled, and his blue eyes, always filled with curiosity, lit up as he saw me. He sported a white t-shirt and a pair of khaki shorts that revealed his sun-kissed skin and toned arms and legs. "Benjamin's here already, helping with dinner."

I turned to see Benjamin standing by the dining table, bottle of wine in hand. Though tall, he seemed to shrink under the weight of his slipping glasses. "Hi, Emma. Hope you don't mind me invading your evening," he said with a nervous laugh.

"Not at all, Benjamin. It's good to see you." I set Oliver down so he could run to his play area. "What's on the menu tonight?"

Daniel chuckled, gesturing toward the kitchen. "Steak and salad. Benjamin brought his famous dressing."

As we moved into the kitchen, the sharp scent of black pepper hung over the hissing steaks. On the counter, an array of vegetables glimmered under the lights. Benjamin sliced tomatoes, the knife gliding through their ripe flesh.

"Look like you guys have everything under control here," I said, leaning against the counter.

"Why don't you go change? Dinner will be ready soon," Daniel said with a grin.

Eager to slip out of my work clothes, I headed to our bedroom. The sounds of chopping and laughter followed me, mixing with Oliver's babble as he recounted his day in the garbled language only a two-year-old could master.

When I returned, the table was set. We gathered around the table as Daniel poured the wine. Benjamin raised his glass. "To good friends and good food!" We echoed his toast.

I cut a steak into bite-sized pieces, making sure they were the right size for Oliver. He watched, his small hands fidgeting with excitement at the sight of the savory meat. "Here we go." I handed him a fork, loaded with tender steak.

"Thanks, Mommy."

"You're welcome, little man." I reached over and ruffled his hair.

"Do you like Dad's steak, Ollie?" Daniel asked across the table.

"Yes," Oliver nodded, mouth full.

I mixed some salad on Oliver's plate and watched as he tentatively poked at the greens. I slipped a small piece of lettuce into his mouth, and his face lit up with surprise and pleasure at the new texture.

"So, how did the repair go today?" Daniel asked, pulling my attention back to the adult conversation. He was always attuned to the daily dramas of the bookstore.

"The pipe's fixed, but the drywall's still a mess," I explained, dabbing my mouth with a napkin. "I'll need to call someone to sort it out. Hopefully, it won't be too much of a hassle."

Benjamin chimed in with a twinkle in his eye. "You think that's bad? You should have seen the winter my parents' house had a pipe burst. The water froze midway through the break and turned half the basement into an ice skating rink!"

Laughter erupted around the table. I pictured Benjamin, usually so composed, skating around a frozen basement, dodging furniture and frozen water jets. Even Oliver giggled, picking up on the mirth without understanding the story.

"It must have been a sight," Daniel said, still chuckling.

"Oh, it was a complete disaster at the time, but looking back, it's one of our funniest family stories."

The steak Daniel had prepared melted in my mouth, expertly seared to lock in all the mouthwatering flavors. "This steak is cooked perfectly, hubby," I praised.

"I tried a new marinade," he said, his smile broadening.

"Daniel, did you hear about the recent donation to the School of Engineering?" Benjamin asked. "Gregory Hale, the alumnus who owns the Hale Construction, just made another donation of $50,000."

"Really? That's impressive," I said. Gregory Hale was a prominent figure in town, respected not only for his thriving business but also for his contributions to local charities.

"It's a generous sum." Daniel nodded. "It should help fund new projects and scholarships for the students."

"As long as it spruces up the University, I'm not complaining," Benjamin chuckled.

I found myself nodding along, touched by the notion of giving back to one's community in such a significant way.

"Could you jog my memory a bit, how did you two meet?" I tried to steer the conversation to a lighter territory.

"Oh gosh, it's been so long I can barely remember," Benjamin said, tapping his chin as if deep in thought.

Daniel shook his head, smiling. "It was five years ago at new employee orientation. I was running late that morning and ended up sitting next to Benjamin. I was frazzled trying to get my materials in order, but he cracked some joke that made me laugh and broke the ice."

"That's right!" Benjamin exclaimed. "I said, 'Welcome to the madhouse!' when they handed us that huge packet of HR forms. Daniel laughed so hard he spilled his coffee."

"It wasn't *that* funny," Daniel said wryly.

"After that, we just hit it off. Found out we were both in the sciences, bonded over being newbies. We grabbed lunch together that day and the rest is history," Benjamin recounted.

Chapter 3

June 18th

The sudden shrill of my phone pierced through the peaceful morning, jolting me and Daniel from sleep. The bright sun peeked through the curtains. I reached for the phone, my heart sinking as I noted the time. I must have overslept because of the wine from last night.

"Emma," Addison, my neighbor's voice crackled through the speaker. "You need to come to Riverside Park. Now!"

Rubbing the sleep from my eyes, I sat up, alarmed by her tone. "Addison, what's happened? Why do you need me there?"

Her next words froze me to the core. "It's Alice. I was jogging by the river... Emma, I found a body. It's Alice."

My breath hitched. "Alice?" The name came out as a whisper, a plea for this to be some terrible mistake.

Daniel stirred beside me. "What's wrong?"

"I... I have to go," I managed to stammer, throwing off the covers. The room seemed to spin as I stood, my legs shaky.

"Emma, I've already called the police. They're on their way. Please hurry," Addison urged.

"Stay where you are, Addison. I'm coming." I dressed quickly, my movements robotic. I grabbed my keys and headed for the door, with Daniel trailing behind me.

As Daniel and I rushed out of the house, the crisp morning air hit me like a splash of cold water. We were halfway to the car when a piercing thought stopped me in my tracks. Oliver.

"We can't leave Oliver alone," I blurted out.

Daniel paused. "Right, of course."

I could see the reluctance in his eyes, the protective instinct that made him want to be by my side, especially now. "You need to stay with Oliver, Dan. I'll go to the park."

"Okay, babe. I will wait until Oliver is awake and then come over with him. Call me the moment you know more."

"I will." I forced a reassuring smile before getting into the car.

The drive to Riverside Park was quick. My mind raced with images of Alice—her laughter, her plans for the summer, the swim we never got to take. *Was this a Joke?*

As I pulled into the park, the sight of police cars and an ambulance in the distance made everything suddenly very real. I walked toward the riverbank, my steps automatic.

The police tape seemed to stretch endlessly, fluttering in the morning breeze, a barrier between the ordinary world and the grim reality just beyond.

Addison stood by the riverbank, her jogging clothes stained with mud, her face pale and drawn. She rushed over as soon as she saw me, her eyes filled with tears.

"I'm so sorry, Emma," she whispered, embracing me tightly. "I didn't know what else to do."

I nodded, my throat tight with grief. "I can't believe Alice is gone," I managed to say, though every word was a struggle against the sob threatening to break free.

I peered across the expanse that separated me from where Alice lay motionless. My eyes strained through the morning light, desperate for a clearer view, but she was just a distant, still form on the riverbank, surrounded by officers combing the area.

The memory of Alice's voice echoed in my mind. Just yesterday, she had been so vibrant, urging me to join her for a swim right here in this park. Guilt gnawed at me, bitter and suffocating. If only I had come with her, perhaps she wouldn't be lying there now. Maybe I could have changed things. The thought clung to me, a dark whisper that I couldn't silence.

Tears blurred my vision. I sobbed, my body shaking with each breath, the sound muffled by the hand I pressed against my mouth. "Please," I managed to choke out to the nearest officer. "I need to see Alice. Just once more. Please."

The officer, a kind-faced woman, approached me with a sympathetic expression. "I'm sorry, ma'am. We're still investigating the scene. I can't let anyone through right now."

"She's my best friend," I stammered, the words tumbling out between sobs. "I need to say goodbye. Please."

The officer's eyes softened and she reached out, placing a hand on my shoulder. "I understand how hard this must be, but we need to preserve the area as best we can. As soon as we've gathered all the necessary evidence, we will let you know."

Her attempt at comfort felt empty against the intense sorrow that engulfed me. The barrier of police tape stood between me and a reality I couldn't accept. Driven by a desperate, wild hope, I ducked under the yellow police tape and ran toward Alice. My only thought was to reach her, to somehow wake her from this nightmare.

"Emma, stop!" I heard Addison's voice echoing behind me and the urgent cries of the police officers, but they were muffled by the pounding of my heart and the deafening rush of blood in my ears.

Reaching Alice, I threw myself over her body, my hands trembling as I touched her cold face. "Alice, it's Emma, please," I sobbed, my voice cracking. "Please, open your eyes."

The officers reached me, their hands gentle but firm as they tried to pull me away. "Ma'am, you need to calm down," one of them said.

But I clung to Alice, my tears spilling onto her still face. "Just give me a moment, please, just a moment," I begged, my voice hoarse with grief.

They hesitated, perhaps understanding the depth of my despair, and allowed me those precious seconds with Alice. As I held her, my hand brushed against her shoulder, and I noticed something unusual—a distinct swelling and discoloration that hadn't been there before. My heart skipped, confusion mingling with my grief. *What had happened to her?*

"We need to preserve the scene, ma'am," an officer said, his tone gentle. "We're not sure yet if this was an accident or something else. We can't have the area disturbed." His words pulled me back to the grim reality.

As I stood, supported by the officers, I took one last look at Alice, the swelling on her shoulder burning into my memory. *What had caused that injury? Something wasn't right.*

The officers led me back behind the police tape, as a detective arrived on the scene. He was of medium height but his muscular, wide-built frame commanded immediate attention. His dark hair was cut short, and his piercing eyes scanned the area with a practiced intensity. He spoke briefly with the officers and turned toward me. I wiped the remnants of tears from my cheeks, steeling myself for the conversation.

"I'm Detective Brown," he introduced himself. "Do you happen to know the deceased?"

"Yes, Detective. My name is Emma Wilson, and I was a friend of Alice Monroe. I need to tell you something. Alice, she was a strong swimmer. And there—there is swelling on her right shoulder. It wasn't like that yesterday."

Detective Brown regarded me with a neutral expression, jotting down notes in his small, worn notebook. "Swelling, you said?"

"Yes, and it looked recent. Alice could swim across this river without breaking a sweat. I don't understand how she could drown."

He nodded slowly. "We'll take all factors into consideration, Ms." He gave me his business card and turned to walk away, signaling to the coroner's team as they prepared to move Alice's body.

"Please wait," I called out to him. "Is there a chance that this wasn't an accident?"

Detective Brown stopped and turned back. "Based on the preliminary evidence and the circumstances, it appears to be an accidental drowning. It's tragic, but these things can happen, even to strong swimmers."

"But the swelling—"

"Could be from a number of things," he interrupted. "We'll look into it, but for now, we have no reason to suspect foul play."

***

Daniel arrived at the park just as the coroner's team zipped up the body bag. He held Oliver in his arms. Oliver's face was buried in his father's neck and his small hands gripped Daniel's t-shirt. The sight of them pierced through the tumult of emotions I was experiencing, and I rushed toward them.

When I embraced them both, Oliver lifted his head and looked at me. "Mommy, why are you crying?"

The innocence of his question tightened the lump in my throat. I kissed his cheek, trying to muster a smile. "It's nothing for you to worry about, sweetheart. Mommy's just a little sad today."

Daniel gave me a look of deep empathy, his hand reaching up to gently stroke my back. "How are you holding up, babe."

I leaned into Daniel's touch for a moment of solace. "It's just so hard to process everything right now."

Daniel's hand found mine and gave it a reassuring squeeze.

"Dan, there's something not right about Alice's shoulder. It looks swollen, and I'm worried it could be a sign of foul play."

"Foul play? Do you really think someone hurt her? Have you told the police?"

"I told Detective Brown of my suspicions, but he thinks that given the current evidence, it's most likely an accidental drowning."

"It's strange that a strong swimmer like Alice would drown in this calm water," Daniel said.

"What should we do?"

"We can't interfere with the police investigation, babe. Let's go home. We'll have plenty of time to find out what happened to Alice."

I nodded. We watched the police and the coroner's team transport Alice's body to the van, taking her for the autopsy that would, I hoped, provide some answers. The van's doors closed with a soft thud.

"Is Auntie Alice sleeping in there?" Oliver asked, pointing toward the van.

I caught Daniel's eyes, unable to speak. "Yes, Ollie, Auntie Alice is resting," Daniel said gently.

We walked back to the car with Oliver between us, his small hand in mine. The park, once a place of joyful visits, now held a shadow over it, a reminder of what had been lost.

Chapter 4

The drive to Mary's house was somber. As I pulled into the driveway, I saw the familiar garden filled with Alice's favorite flowers. The bright colors seemed to mock the sorrow that hung in the air. When Mary, Alice's mother, opened the door, her red-rimmed eyes and sorrow-filled face pulled a sob from my chest. We fell into each other's arms, our embrace tight and desperate.

We made our way inside and took a seat in the living room. Photographs of Alice adorned the walls: moments of joy and life. Seeing those images only highlighted the fact that she was no longer with us. "I should have been with Alice, Mary. I should have gone swimming with her, but my bookstore was flooded and I thought I would go with her next week," I confessed, the words heavy with regret. "Maybe I could have done something. Maybe she'd still be here."

Tears streamed down my cheeks, the burden of 'what ifs' overwhelming. Mary reached out, her hand gripping mine with a strength that belied her gentle appearance.

"Emma, you can't do this to yourself. Alice loved swimming, and it was her choice to go yesterday morning. You couldn't have known what would happen. We can't live our lives based on what we think we should have done."

Her words, meant to console, did little to lift the weight from my shoulders, but the kindness in her eyes, the understanding of a mother's love, brought me comfort. "It's just so hard, Mary. I miss her so much," I managed to say, the words choked by sobs.

Mary pulled me into another embrace. "I know, darling, I know," she murmured, rocking slightly as we held each other. "I miss her every moment. But we have to remember the good times with her and cherish the love she brought into our lives. We have to be strong—for her."

We sat together for a long time. After our tears had dried a bit and a silence settled between us, I gathered the courage to broach a topic that had been pressing heavily on my mind. "Mary, have the police given you any updates about... about what happened to Alice?"

Mary shook her head. "No, nothing. They said they would perform an autopsy, but that was all."

I leaned in closer. "Have you noticed anything unusual about Alice lately?"

"Alice was always such a positive person, but recently I noticed she was under some kind of stress. She tried to hide it, but a mother knows when something's wrong."

My heart ached at the thought of Alice struggling alone. "Did she say what was bothering her? Was it work-related or something in her personal life?"

Mary shook her head. "She didn't tell me, Emma. I asked her several times, but she just brushed it off, saying it was nothing she couldn't handle. I wish she had confided in me."

"Alice was strong, but she shouldn't have had to deal with whatever it was on her own. I've been preoccupied with the bookstore recently. I should have talked to her more." I hesitated, the next words sticking in my throat as I considered whether to share my concerns. But Mary deserved to know. "When I found Alice, there was swelling on her right shoulder. It looked unusual, like an injury."

Mary's eyes widened, a flicker of alarm passing through them. "An injury? Do you think someone harmed her?"

"I don't know, but I'm worried it might be foul play. The police seem to think it was just an accident, a drowning, but it doesn't sit right with me."

Mary's hands clenched into fists. "If someone hurt my girl, I want to know why. Emma, you were Alice's closest friend. Please, if someone harmed Alice, I need you to find the person responsible. I know it's a lot to ask, but I know you have the strength to give Alice the justice she deserves."

I nodded. "I will, Mary. Alice was like a sister to me. I owe her that much."

Mary reached out, her hand gripping mine. "I know you'll do everything for Alice."

Chapter 5

It had been days since Alice's body was found in Riverside Park, and the lack of updates about the cause of her death left me in a fog of frustration.

Victoria was restocking a shelf nearby when she turned to me. "Emma, can I ask you something?"

"Of course. What's on your mind?" I closed the ledger I had been working on.

"How did you and Alice become such good friends? You've talked about her a lot, but I don't think I've ever heard the whole story."

I leaned back in my chair, a smile tugging at my lips as memories flooded back. "We met during our first week at the University. I was a nervous freshman, majoring in history, and Alice was this vibrant journalism major. We ended up in the same dorm and quickly bonded over late-night study sessions."

Victoria smiled. "So you became friends right away?"

"Pretty much. Alice had this infectious energy that drew people to her. She was passionate about her studies and had a knack for uncovering the truth, even back then. We became roommates in our sophomore year, and that's when we really grew close."

I paused, reminiscing about those early days. "Alice loved swimming. She said it was the one thing that helped her clear her mind. She insisted on teaching me how to swim, even though I was terrified at first. She was patient, though, and eventually, I fell in love with swimming as well. We'd go to the campus pool almost every week."

Victoria's eyes sparkled with interest. "She sounds like she was a wonderful friend."

"She was. Alice was my bridesmaid when I married Daniel. She stood by my side, helping me through all the chaos and excitement of wedding planning. She even managed to keep me calm on the big day, which was no small feat."

I laughed softly at the memory, and Victoria joined in. "It seems like you two were more like sisters than friends."

"Yes, exactly. Alice was like a sister to me. We shared so many milestones and supported each other through everything. Losing her has been... incredibly hard."

"I'm sorry, Emma. I can't imagine how difficult this must be for you."

"Talking about her helps keep her memory alive. And it reminds me why it's so important to find out what happened to her," I said, giving her a grateful smile.

"Maybe a little distraction could help?" Victoria gestured to the stack of newly arrived mystery novels in her hands.

"What do you have there?"

"Well, I thought maybe we could do a little display. 'Mysteries that take us around the world'—something to stir up the wanderlust in our customers," Victoria suggested.

"That's interesting." I took the books from her and examined the covers.

We arranged the books on a front table, carefully positioning them next to a globe and some travel-themed decor items.

***

In my office, I found Detective Brown's business card tucked away in the depths of my purse. I dialed the number, the dial tone echoing loudly in the still air.

"Detective Brown speaking."

"Detective Brown, Good morning! It's Emma Wilson. Alice Monroe's friend. I was hoping you could update me on the investigation into Alice's death."

There was a pause, and when he spoke again, Detective Brown's tone was dismissive. "Ms., I can't discuss details of the investigation, especially not with someone who isn't family."

"She is my best friend, Detective. We were college roommates. I care for Alice and wish to know what happened to my friend. There was swelling on her shoulder, something was wrong—"

"Ms., I understand you're upset," he interrupted, his voice stern, "but I have to follow protocol. We'll release information to the public when it's appropriate. Until then, there's nothing I can say."

The dismissal in his tone ignited a spark of anger within me. "It's been days without any updates. I'm afraid someone might have harmed her. Is there anything I can do to assist with the investigation?"

"Ms., police investigations take time," he responded, his tone more clipped now. "Jumping to conclusions won't help. Let us handle this. That's what we're trained for."

"Detective, I just want to know if there has been any progress. How can I just sit back and do nothing if the investigation stalls?" I exclaimed.

His voice trembles with barely contained rage as he spits out the words, "I have nothing else to say to you. Don't call me again."

I stood there, phone in hand, the dial tone echoing through the quiet bookstore like a lonely cry.

Chapter 6

The bell above the door chimed. When I looked up from the counter, I was surprised to see Wyatt walking in. My brother's presence always brought me joy.

"Wyatt." I came around the counter to greet him. "I didn't expect to see you today."

He opened his arms wide for a hug, which I gladly stepped into. "Good afternoon, Emma. We just got back from vacation."

Pulling back, I looked up at him. "How are Susan and the boys? Noah and James must have grown since I last saw them."

"Susan is doing well, and the boys are good. Noah's knee-deep in his science projects, and James has just started soccer practice," Wyatt replied, his eyes lighting up with paternal pride. "They keep asking when they can visit Aunt Emma's bookstore again."

I laughed. "Tell them anytime. I might recruit them to help me organize the children's section."

Wyatt's expression became more serious. "How are you holding up? I heard about what happened to Alice. I'm so sorry, Emma. If there's anything I can do—"

"Actually, there is something. Maybe you can help me understand something Detective Brown seems to be overlooking," I said.

Wyatt and I made our way to the reading nook in the back and took a seat. He was a senior detective at the Athens Police Department. I wanted to involve him in my search for the truth about Alice, but at the same time, I didn't want to burden him with my problems.

Wyatt's detective instincts kicked in. "Tell me everything, Emma."

I shared my concerns about the circumstances surrounding Alice's death, including her exceptional swimming ability and the mysterious swelling on her shoulder. Wyatt listened intently, as he pieced together the information.

My voice shook as I admitted, "I don't believe Detective Brown's theory that it was an accidental drowning. There's more to this, and I need to find out what really happened, for Alice's sake."

A tear slipped down my cheek as I continued. "I keep thinking—if only I had gone swimming with her that morning, maybe she'd still be here." The confession broke from me in a rush, the familiar guilt that had shadowed much of my life resurfacing, bitter and accusing.

Wyatt leaned back in his chair. "Emma, you said the exact same thing when Mom and Dad died. You know, it's been years since we talked about Mom and Dad's accident."

I nodded, feeling a familiar pang of sadness. "I know. It's always hard to bring it up, but I think about it all the time."

Wyatt sighed, looking out the window as if lost in the past. "I remember that day so clearly. I was fifteen, trying to act tough and grown-up, but when we got the news… it felt like the world ended."

I swallowed hard, memories flooding back. "I was only ten. I begged them to buy me that Barbie doll. On their way home, they were hit by a drunk driver. If I hadn't—"

Wyatt took my hand in his. "Emma, you have to stop blaming yourself. You were a kid. It wasn't your fault."

"But if I hadn't begged for the Barbie doll, they wouldn't have been on the road. They wouldn't have been hit by that drunk driver."

Wyatt's grip tightened. "It was the drunk driver's fault, not yours. You were just a little girl who wanted a doll. You can't carry that guilt forever."

Tears welled up in my eyes as I looked at my brother. "I know you're right, but it's hard to let go. We lost them because of something I wanted."

Wyatt's face softened, and he leaned closer. "Emma, I see you struggling with the same feelings of guilt with Alice's death. But it wasn't your fault then, and it's not your fault now. These tragedies... you couldn't have prevented them."

I looked away, staring out the window. "I know, logically, I know that," I murmured. But the pain from our parents' accident years ago had resurfaced in the last few days, feeling just as fresh and raw as ever. "But it feels like if I had just made different choices..."

Wyatt squeezed my hand, bringing me back. "Guilt is a heavy burden to carry, Emma, and it's a deceptive one. It can make you feel responsible for things beyond your control. You can't carry this burden for Alice's death. We need to find out what happened, yes, but not because you owe it to your guilt. We do it because Alice deserves the truth, and because you deserve peace."

His words fortified me. The tears that had threatened now seemed to recede a bit, like the tide pulling back from the shore. "I'm so glad you're here, Wyatt. Can you help me to investigate what happened to Alice that morning?"

I could see the hesitation in Wyatt's eyes.

"Emma, it's Detective Brown's case. I don't want to step on any toes or strain relationships at the department."

"But you know I can't just let this go," I insisted, my voice firm and desperate. "Please, Wyatt."

We sat in silence, the overhead light creating shadows that only added to the weight of our conversation. Wyatt looked around, perhaps ensuring our privacy, before leaning forward.

"I get it, Emma. I truly do. Alice has been a part of your life since you were roommates in college and I care about her too. If I'm going to help you, we need to do this the right way." His voice was resolute. "I'll take you to the coroner's office and we can take a look at the autopsy report together. I hope seeing the report will bring you some closure and calm your mind."

Hope surged through me, but before I could respond, he held up a hand to stop me.

"But, I need to ask Detective Brown for permission first. I have to make sure we're not overstepping or interfering with the ongoing investigation."

"Of course. I just need to know what really happened."

"I know how stubborn you can be, little sis. I'll talk to Detective Brown first thing in the morning. We'll go from there." Wyatt stood, moving toward the door.

***

The soft hum of the air conditioning and the quiet rustle of pages turning created a peaceful atmosphere in the bookstore. I was organizing a display of new arrivals when my phone buzzed in my pocket. Seeing Daniel's name on the screen, I smiled and answered.

"Hey, hubby, how's everything going?"

There was a brief pause, and I felt a knot of worry form in my stomach. "Emma," Daniel began, his voice strained. "I have some bad news. It's about Mom."

"What happened? Is she okay?"

"Mom's been diagnosed with melanoma. It's skin cancer. The doctors say she needs surgery and probably chemotherapy afterward."

The world seemed to tilt for a moment, and I had to steady myself against the bookshelf. "Oh my God, Daniel. How bad is it?"

"They caught it relatively early. But it's still serious."

I tried to process the information. Margaret had always been so strong. The thought of her facing cancer was almost too much to bear. "When will be the surgery?"

"They're scheduling it for next week," Daniel said. "I'm going to take some time off to be with her and Dad in Atlanta. They could use all the support they can get."

"Of course. Oliver and I will join you on the weekend. We will be there for them."

Chapter 7

Wyatt pulled up outside my bookstore, and I climbed into the passenger seat beside him.

"Detective Brown has agreed to let me help with the case. I'll take you to meet with Dr. Henry Jones, the coroner handling Alice's autopsy."

"That's great!"

"Dr. Jones should have finished the autopsy and toxicology reports by now."

Located just outside of Athens, the coroner's office was a beige one-story building, with a small sign above the door that read "County Coroner." The parking lot was nearly empty, with a few cars scattered across the asphalt. The building was bordered by a sparse line of trees that offered a modicum of privacy.

We approached the entrance, I caught a glimpse of my nervous expression reflected in the glass door. Inside, the walls were painted a calming shade of blue. A small reception desk sat to one side, manned by a middle-aged woman with a kind face.

"Good afternoon," she greeted us with a polite smile. "How can I help you?"

Wyatt flashed his badge. "Detective Wyatt Miller. We're here to see Dr. Henry Jones about a case."

"Of course, Detective Miller. Dr. Jones is expecting you. Please, follow me."

We followed her down a narrow hallway, the fluorescent lights overhead casting a sterile glow on the linoleum floor. The corridor was lined with doors, each marked with simple plaques indicating various examination and storage rooms. The faint scent of antiseptic lingered in the air.

At the end of the hallway, she knocked on a door labeled "Dr. Henry Jones, Coroner." A moment later, it opened to reveal a man in his late fifties, his salt-and-pepper hair neatly combed and his eyes sharp behind a pair of wire-rimmed glasses.

"Detective Miller, Ms. Wilson," he greeted us. "Please, come in."

We stepped into his office, a small but orderly room filled with filing cabinets. A large desk dominated the space, cluttered with papers and reports. A computer screen displayed various charts and data.

Dr. Jones motioned for us to sit. "I understand you have some questions about the case involving Alice Monroe."

"Yes," Wyatt began. "We're hoping you can provide us with some insight based on your findings."

"I'm sorry for your loss, Ms. Wilson. I'll share what I can," Dr. Jones said.

"You can call me Emma."

"I've completed a thorough examination of Alice Monroe's body, and there's something you both need to know," Dr. Jones said, his expression grave.

My heart pounded in my chest. "What did you find, Dr. Jones?"

He took a deep breath, folding his hands on the desk. "Toxicology reports show that Alice had a significant amount of ketamine and xylazine in her system. Ketamine and xylazine are animal tranquilizers."

"Animal tranquilizers?"

"Yes. Ketamine and xylazine are commonly used to subdue wild animals and are also used in zoos to sedate animals. Additionally, I found two small puncture wounds on her body: one on her back and another on her right shoulder. Given the concentration of the tranquilizers and the puncture wounds on her body, I believe Alice was shot with an animal dart gun."

"So, you're saying someone injected her with animal tranquilizers?" Wyatt asked.

"Precisely. These tranquilizers are typically used for large animals. The dosage was enough to sedate an animal several times Alice's size."

I felt sick to my stomach. "But why? Who would someone do such a thing?"

Wyatt and Dr. Jones exchanged a look. "It's clear this wasn't an accident," Wyatt said slowly. "Alice was murdered. This is now a homicide investigation."

"Yes, I believe so. The puncture wounds are unmistakable, and the tranquilizers indicate a clear intent to harm," Dr. Jones said.

"Do we know what kind of dart gun was used?" Wyatt asked.

Dr. Jones shook his head. "Not yet, but the wounds suggest a high-powered dart gun, the kind typically used in zoos or wildlife preserves."

"An animal dart gun and animal tranquilizers are not something you can easily get your hands on," Wyatt said.

Dr. Jones nodded in agreement. "An animal dart gun can be obtained relatively easily through online or retail stores, but animal tranquilizers are controlled substances. Only licensed veterinarians can prescribe and administer these drugs. Veterinarians must maintain meticulous records of their use and storage, and they are subject to periodic inspections by regulatory authorities. Animal tranquilizers are typically used by veterinarians, zoo personnel, or wildlife researchers."

A surge of anger coursed through me. "So, Alice was shot with animal tranquilizers and then drowned."

"That's what it looks like," Dr. Jones confirmed. "The tranquilizers would have taken effect quickly, making it impossible for her to keep swimming."

"Were you able to locate the darts that were used on Alice?" I asked.

"No, there were no darts found on Alice's body, and they were not present at the scene. It appears that Alice pulled the darts out before drowning," Dr. Jones replied.

Wyatt leaned back in his chair, his brow furrowed in thought. "We need to figure out who in the area has access to these animal tranquilizers."

Dr. Jones tapped his fingers on the desk. "There are a few veterinarians in the area who might have the necessary equipment and access to these animal tranquilizers. Additionally, there are the Athens Zoo and several wildlife rehabilitation centers nearby."

Wyatt pulled out his notebook and began jotting down notes. "We'll need to check with local suppliers too. See who's been purchasing these kinds of tranquilizers recently. We've got work to do." Wyatt stood up and thanked Dr. Jones for his time.

"Thank you, doctor. Alice would appreciate all your help." I hugged Dr. Jones before walking out of his office.

"Alice loved swimming," I said as we stepped outside the building. "During the summer, she went at least twice a week, usually to the same spot at Riverside Park. I think someone must have ambushed her there with an animal dart gun."

"The water at Riverside Park is so calm and shallow," Wyatt said slowly. "It's hard to imagine someone setting up an ambush in the middle of the river. How could they have done it?"

I thought back to the countless times Alice and I had spent at Riverside Park, swimming, chatting, and enjoying the peace of nature. The thought that this peaceful place could become a crime scene seemed unbelievable.

"Maybe someone watched her," I reasoned. "They knew her routine, knew where she swam. If they used a boat or hid along the riverbank, they could have hit her with a dart when she was swimming."

"You may be right," Wyatt said, though the doubt in his voice was evident. "But it still seems like such a risky move. Ambushing someone in broad daylight in a public place. The area is too open, especially during the day… it's bold, and it suggests they knew what they were doing."

After we climbed into his car, Wyatt said, "I'll bring up these new findings when I speak with Detective Brown. I believe our investigation should begin with the animal tranquilizer lead."

"How long do you think it will take for the police to catch Alice's killer?" I asked.

Wyatt sighed as he started the car. "I don't know, Emma. The department is really busy right now, and I don't want you to set your expectations too high. We'll investigate, but these things take time."

His words felt like a cold slap of reality. The thought of Alice's killer walking free was unbearable. "I can't just wait and hope for the best," I said.

"I know, Emma. But we have to be realistic. The department has a lot of cases to handle, and we can't prioritize one over the other just because it's personal."

I bit my lip, my frustration mounting. "You know what? I'll investigate it myself. I knew Alice better than anyone, and I'll find out who did this to her."

Wyatt glanced at me. "Emma, you need to be careful. If someone murdered Alice, they might not hesitate to hurt you, too."

"I can't pretend that everything is okay. I can't let someone take Alice away from me like that. That is not a life I am willing to live."

Wyatt sighed, "I should not have taken you to see Dr. Jones. Just promise me you'll be careful. And if you find anything, you come to me first."

"I promise."

Chapter 8

Daniel and I walked along the gravel path of Riverside Park, the afternoon sun beating down on us. We arrived at the familiar spot where Alice loved to swim. It was a peaceful section of the river. The gentle flow of the river caused the sunlight to dance on its surface, creating a mesmerizing atmosphere. The grassy bank was soft, and a few large rocks protruded from the water, perfect for sitting and dipping your feet in.

Today, the usual crowd was absent. Only a pair of teenagers relaxed on the riverbank, and an older man sat on a boulder, gazing thoughtfully at the rippling water. I suspected the sparse crowd was due to the recent tragedy of Alice's drowning. The town was still recovering from the unexpected loss.

We changed into our swimsuits and approached the river. "Alice loved this spot," I murmured, more to myself than to Daniel.

"Are you sure you want to do this?" Daniel asked as he took my hand.

"I need to."

We waded into the water, the gentle current lapping against our legs. The water was cool and inviting. For a moment, the joy of being in the water almost made me forget why we were there.

Following the path I knew Alice often took, I began to swim, Daniel close beside me. I allowed myself to recall the happy times Alice and I shared in this very spot, laughing and talking as we swam together.

We swam toward the middle of the river, where Alice liked to linger, and I tried to imagine where someone could have ambushed her. The water was only about chest-deep, and clear enough that I could see the riverbed below. It seemed impossible that anyone could approach her unnoticed with a dart gun.

"Maybe they hid along the riverbank," I suggested, treading water as I looked around. "But how would they have gotten a clear shot from there?"

"Or maybe from a boat," Daniel said, looking around. "It would explain how they managed to get close enough to use a dart gun."

My mind raced with the possibilities. I realized how exposed we were in the water. Anyone on the shore or a boat nearby could have seen Alice easily, especially if they knew her routine.

As Daniel and I began to swim back to shore, I noticed we were slowly drifting downstream, carried by the gentle but persistent current. I paused to look around, feeling a subtle tug of concern as we were farther from our starting point than I'd anticipated.

"Hey, Dan," I called out, turning my head toward him. "We're drifting downstream. We should start heading back to shore."

He nodded, and we both adjusted our strokes. I noticed a couple of places along the riverbank where the trees and bushes were particularly dense. The overhanging branches and thick foliage created natural hiding spots, secluded and shadowy.

"Look at those trees." I pointed at the dense patches. "It's possible someone could have hidden there and hit Alice with a dart."

Daniel stopped swimming and looked where I was pointing. The trees seemed to lean over the water, their branches providing ample cover for someone lurking there.

"From those spots, someone could have ambushed her easily, especially if she wasn't paying attention," Daniel agreed.

We swam toward the areas where the bushes were thickest. I trod water for a moment, examining the bank. The patches were secluded, offering both cover and a clear line of sight to where Alice swam. The scenario made my heart ache; imagining my friend's last moments, defenseless and unaware.

Once we reached the riverbank, we sat on the grass, catching our breath. "Someone must have been watching her, studying her schedule and routine," I said. "They must have planned this."

"And they were cunning enough to make it look like an accident," Daniel added.

We sat in silence for a while, watching the river flow gently by, its calm surface belying the tragedy it had recently witnessed.

Daniel glanced at me. "Emma, maybe we should just leave this to the police. We don't have any experience with murder investigations. It's dangerous."

I looked out over the water. The idea of sitting idly by, waiting for the police to untangle the web of Alice's murder, was unbearable. "I can't just sit on my hands and wait, Dan. I need to do something."

"The person who did this is cunning and resourceful. What if you get too close and they come after you next?"

"Well, you married a headstrong woman, didn't you?" I joked, trying to lighten the mood.

Daniel couldn't suppress a small smile. "That I did. But that doesn't mean I want to risk losing you."

Reaching out, I took his hand and squeezed it gently. "You are not going to lose me, Dan. But I have to follow this through, for Alice. She would have done the same for me."

I leaned toward him, resting my head on his broad shoulder. Daniel's firm hand grasped my waist, drawing me in closer to him. I could feel the heat radiating from his large hand.

"Do you remember how we first met?" I asked.

"How could I forget? It was about four years ago, right here in Riverside Park. Benjamin and I were jogging, trying to get in shape for that charity run."

The memory came back to me vividly. "Alice and I were swimming in the river. It was a sunny day."

"Yeah," Daniel said, his eyes twinkling. "I saw two beautiful girls in the water, and I couldn't take my eyes off the brunette who turned out to be you."

I nudged him playfully. "You mean the girl you almost drowned trying to talk to."

"In my defense, I didn't know swimming wasn't one of my strengths until that moment. I thought, 'How hard can it be?'"

"You swallowed mouthfuls of water," I teased, remembering the sight of him struggling as he swam toward us.

"And you laughed at me. You made a joke about how I should've brought a life jacket."

"I couldn't help it," I said, smiling. "You were so determined and so clearly out of your depth. But it was sweet. You didn't give up, even when Benjamin tried to drag you back to shore."

Daniel took my hand in his. "I couldn't give up. I had to meet you. Something about you just drew me in."

I felt a warm flush spread through me, the memory of that day blending with the deep love I felt for him now. "I'm so glad you did. Who knew that day would lead us here?"

He pulled me closer, wrapping his arm around my shoulders. "Fate has a funny way of working things out. Meeting you was the best thing that ever happened to me."

We sat there in comfortable silence for a moment, watching the river flow by.

"I miss Alice," I said. "She was there that day, too. She laughed at you just as much as I did."

"She was a good friend. I know how much she meant to you, Emma."

I leaned my head against his shoulder, finding strength.

Chapter 9

On the day of Alice's funeral, the sky was overcast, a gloomy gray that reflected the sadness weighing on the hearts of everyone in attendance. The service was held at a small, white church just outside of town, its steeple reaching toward the sky as if pleading for Alice's soul.

Mary sat in the front row, her shoulders shaking with silent sobs. I could hardly bear to see her like this, the pain of losing her only child visible on her face. Daniel and I took our seats a few rows back, as I struggled to hold back my tears.

Alice's colleagues from Athens Chronicle, the town's newspaper, sat nearby, a blend of sadness and admiration on their faces. They had placed a large wreath of white lilies near the altar, a tribute to their fallen coworker. Eleanor and Avery sat beside me, their presence a reminder that I wasn't alone in my grief.

The minister's words were a blur. I barely heard the eulogy, though I knew it spoke of Alice's vibrant spirit, her dedication to her work, and the joy she brought to everyone who knew her. When it was my turn to speak, I rose on unsteady legs, feeling the weight of every eye in the room upon me.

"I met Alice in college," I began, my voice trembling. "She was my roommate, my best friend, and eventually, my sister in every way that mattered. Alice had a way of making everyone feel special, of lighting up a room with her smile. She was fearless in her pursuit of the truth, and she inspired everyone around her to be better, to do better."

I paused, my throat tight with emotion. "Alice's death is a tragedy, but I know she would want us to remember her for the life she lived, not the way she died. She was a force of nature, and she will live on in our hearts and memories forever."

As I stepped down, Mary reached out and squeezed my hand, her eyes filled with gratitude through her tears. The service continued and a series of heartfelt tributes painted a picture of a life well-lived, albeit far too short.

After the service, we made our way to the cemetery. The rain held off just long enough for Alice to be laid to rest. The first drops began to fall as the final words were spoken and the coffin was lowered into the ground. We stood together, united in our sorrow, as the heavens wept with us.

Chapter 10

Later that afternoon, Eleanor, Avery, and I gathered at Marlow's Café, a local restaurant that had been a favorite of Alice's. We settled into a corner booth, the smell of freshly baked bread and brewing coffee mingling with the faint scent of lavender from the small vase of flowers on our table.

Eleanor, always the pragmatic one, adjusted her glasses and peered at me with a lawyer's scrutiny. "Emma, you've been awfully quiet since the service. What's on your mind?"

Avery, her gentle eyes full of concern, reached across the table to squeeze my hand. "You can tell us anything, Emma. We're here for you."

I took a deep breath, feeling the weight of the truth pressing against my chest. "Alice didn't simply drown. She was murdered."

The silence that followed was thick. Eleanor's eyes widened, and Avery gasped, covering her mouth with her hand.

"Murdered? Emma, are you sure?" Eleanor asked.

"Positive. I can't go into all the details, but the police are aware that Alice was injured before she drowned."

"Alice was an Olympic swimmer. Swimming was her sport. She wouldn't have drowned, especially not at Riverside Park," Avery stated with conviction.

"What caused Alice's injury?" Eleanor asked.

"Someone injected her with animal tranquilizers using a dart gun, making it appear as if she drowned accidentally," I explained.

Avery's brow furrowed as she looked between Eleanor and me. "Have the police found the person who did this?"

"I'm not sure how much effort the police are putting into her case."

"Who is leading the investigation into Alice's death?" Eleanor leaned in.

"It's Detective Brown. He initially ruled Alice's death as accidental drowning. But now, whenever I try to contact him, he hangs up on me."

Eleanor nodded, her expression turning serious. "If Alice was murdered, we can't just sit by and do nothing. We need to look into this."

"We owe it to Alice to find out the truth. She was our friend," Avery added.

The waitress arrived with our orders, placing plates of steaming soup and fresh sandwiches in front of us.

"We need to identify potential suspects. Who would have a motive to harm Alice?" I asked, stirring my iced tea absently. "I've been thinking about Jack. Do you think he could have had a motive to murder Alice?"

Eleanor frowned. "They had a nasty breakup a few months ago. I remember Alice telling me how bitter and angry he was. But murder? That seems extreme, even for someone as volatile as Jack."

"I don't know, Eleanor. Breakups can bring out the worst in people, especially if Jack felt humiliated or rejected. Do you remember how possessive he was? Alice said he couldn't stand the thought of her moving on," Avery said.

I nodded, recalling the heated arguments Alice had confided in me about. "He did seem obsessive. He showed up at her apartment unannounced several times, trying to win her back even after she made it clear it was over."

Eleanor sighed, pushing her plate aside. "Would he go so far as to kill her? And if he did, why use such a calculated method? The animal tranquilizer, the staged drowning… it seems more like the work of someone with a plan, not a crime of passion."

"That's true," I admitted. "But maybe he had help or guidance. Or perhaps he thought it would be less suspicious if it looked like an accident."

Avery's eyes narrowed. "Jack works in software engineering. He's smart enough to figure out how to cover his tracks. And he had the motive—anger, jealousy, a bruised ego."

We sat in silence for a moment, each lost in our thoughts.

"Do we know if Jack has any connections to places where he could get animal tranquilizers?" Eleanor asked, breaking the silence.

I shook my head. "Not that I know of. It's something we should look into. If he's involved, he might have found a way to get his hands on them."

Avery took a sip of her coffee. "We also need to consider his alibi. Where was Jack the morning Alice drowned?"

I pulled out my notebook, jotting down our thoughts. "We'll need to talk to him. See if his story checks out. And we should also ask around—maybe someone saw him that day or knows something about his recent behavior."

The soothing hum of Marlow's Café enveloped us as we sat around our corner booth, our lunch half-eaten and forgotten.

Eleanor took a sip of iced water. "Don't forget about Penelope Green. Penelope was always envious of Alice's success. She made no secret of her resentment when Alice got that promotion last year. Could envy push her to murder?"

"Jealousy can make people do terrible things, especially when it's mixed with professional rivalry. Penelope was constantly trying to outdo Alice, always looking for ways to undermine her," Avery added.

I leaned forward, my elbows resting on the table. "Alice mentioned a few times how Penelope would take credit for her ideas or try to sabotage her projects. It was exhausting for Alice, dealing with that kind of hostility every day."

Eleanor sighed, stirring her soup. "Would Penelope go as far as to kill Alice? It's one thing to be competitive and spiteful, but murder is something else entirely."

"That's what we need to figure out," I replied. "We need to look at Penelope's actions and see if there's anything that suggests she could have done this. Did Alice say anything recently about Penelope acting more aggressive?"

Avery bit her lip. "Alice did mention that Penelope was furious about a story Alice was working on. Something big that would have gotten Alice a lot of recognition. Maybe Penelope felt threatened and decided to take drastic measures."

Eleanor nodded in agreement. "You bring up a valid point. If Alice was close to breaking the biggest story of her career, Penelope might have seen it as her last chance to bring Alice down."

I jotted down notes in my notebook. "We need to find out if Penelope had access to animal tranquilizers and a dart gun. It's a long shot, but if she did, it would be a significant lead."

"Penelope is resourceful. She might have connections we don't know about. And she's certainly smart enough to cover her tracks," Avery said.

"We also need to check her alibi for the morning Alice drowned," Eleanor added. "If Penelope has no solid alibi, it would raise even more questions."

"I'll talk to Alice's colleagues at the newspaper. See if they noticed anything unusual about Penelope's behavior recently. Maybe someone saw or heard something that could help us," I said.

Eleanor tapped her chin, considering the possibilities. "We can't rule out anyone at this point. Jack had a personal motive and Penelope had a professional one. Both could be capable of something like this if pushed far enough."

"Alice was a journalist. She must have been working on something recently. Maybe it's related to her work. We need to find out what she was investigating," I said.

"We could start by looking through her notes and her articles. There might be something there that connects to her death," Avery suggested.

"I'll see if I can get access to her work files. Maybe there's a story she was working on that someone wanted to keep quiet," I said.

Avery leaned back, her eyes narrowing in thought. "What about Dr. Harold Bates? Remember what happened with his veterinary clinic after Alice's investigation?"

My mind flashed back to the high-profile case from two years ago. Alice had uncovered a web of animal abuse and neglect at Dr. Bates's clinic. "Right, Dr. Bates. Alice spent months gathering evidence and talking to former employees and pet owners. She even went undercover to get the story."

Eleanor nodded. "I remember the articles and the TV coverage. Alice's reporting was thorough and damning. She exposed how Dr. Bates was mistreating animals, not providing proper care, and overcharging clients. It was a huge scandal."

"And after that," Avery added, "the clinic was shut down, Dr. Bates lost his license, and he was fined heavily. He even faced criminal charges, though I think he got off with probation and community service."

"That's right," I recalled the fallout. "Alice received a lot of praise for her work, but she also got threats. Dr. Bates was furious. He blamed her for ruining his career."

Eleanor leaned in closer, her voice low. "Do you think he could have harbored that resentment for all this time? Enough to kill her?"

"It's possible," I replied. "Losing his clinic and his license must have devastated him. If he blamed Alice for all of it, who knows what he might be capable of?"

Avery looked thoughtful. "Dr. Bates was always a bit off, even before the scandal. I wouldn't put it past him to hold a grudge. And with his background, he would definitely have access to animal tranquilizers."

The pieces started to fit together in a chilling way. Dr. Bates had the motive and the means to harm Alice. "We need to find out what he's been up to since the clinic closed," I said. "If he's still in town, we should see if he's had any run-ins with Alice recently."

Eleanor pulled out her phone. "I'll start looking into his recent activities. There might be something that links him to Alice's death."

I sighed, the weight of the investigation pressing down on me. I took a sip of iced tea and turned to Avery. "So, Avery, how's Jimmy doing these days?" I tried to steer our conversation toward a more lighthearted topic.

Avery smiled, a soft blush coloring her cheeks. "He's good. He's been trying to get into shape lately."

Eleanor raised an eyebrow, a mischievous grin spreading across her face. "Oh? And what's brought on this sudden burst of fitness enthusiasm?"

Avery's blush deepened. "Well, we're trying to get pregnant, and Jimmy wants to be in the best shape possible. You know, to keep up with a little one when the time comes."

I couldn't help but join Eleanor in her teasing. "Really? Getting into shape to keep up with a baby? He knows they don't start running around right away, right?"

Eleanor chuckled. "Yeah, he's got at least a year or so before he has to worry about chasing after a toddler. Maybe he's just trying to impress you, Avery."

Avery rolled her eyes, but her smile showed she appreciated the teasing. "You two are terrible. But honestly, it's sweet. He wants to be the best dad he can be."

"Well, we can't argue with that," I said, reaching over to squeeze her hand. "It's wonderful that you two are preparing for a baby."

Eleanor's eyes twinkled with amusement. "Just make sure he doesn't overdo it. We wouldn't want him to pull a muscle before he even has a chance to change his first diaper."

Avery laughed. "Don't worry, I'll keep him in check. But seriously, this whole trying-to-conceive thing can be stressful, and your humor makes it easier."

"When the time comes, we'll be here for baby showers, babysitting, and all the rest," I said warmly.

Eleanor raised her glass in a mock toast. "To Jimmy's fitness journey and the future baby!"

We clinked our glasses together. For a moment, the heaviness of Alice's death faded into the background.

I glanced over at Eleanor. "So, Eleanor, how's your dating life going?"

Eleanor groaned, setting her fork down. "Oh, don't get me started. My most recent date was an absolute disaster."

Avery leaned in. "What happened?"

Eleanor rolled her eyes. "Well, I met this guy online. He seemed great at first—funny, charming, had a good job. We decided to meet for dinner at that new Italian place midtown."

"Sounds promising so far." I encouraged her to continue.

"Yeah, well, that's where the good part ends. We sit down, and within the first ten minutes, he's already bragging about how much money he makes and how many cars he owns. It was like he was trying to impress me with his bank account instead of, you know, his personality."

Avery winced. "Yikes. That's a big red flag."

"It gets worse. Halfway through the meal, he took a phone call and left me sitting there for fifteen minutes while he talked about some business deal. I ended up eating my pasta alone."

"Oh no, that's terrible! Did you confront him about it?" I asked.

"When he finally came back, I told him how rude it was to leave me sitting there. And do you know what he said?

He said, 'You should be grateful I even showed up. Most women would kill for a chance to go out with me.'"

Avery gasped, and I shook my head in disbelief. "What a jerk! I'm so sorry, Eleanor. You deserve so much better than that."

Eleanor shrugged. "Yeah, well, it's just another bad date to add to the list. I'm starting to think maybe I should take a break from the whole dating scene."

"No way," Avery said firmly. "Don't let one bad apple spoil the whole bunch. There are good guys out there. You just haven't found the right one yet."

"Exactly," I chimed in. "You're an amazing person, Eleanor. The right guy is out there, and he'll appreciate you for who you are."

Eleanor sighed. "I guess it's just frustrating sometimes. You're right. I shouldn't give up."

We raised our glasses in a mock toast. "To Eleanor's future dates—may they be infinitely better than the last one."

Chapter 11

Late afternoon, Eleanor and I pulled into the gas station on the outskirts of town. It was a far cry from the busy veterinary clinic Dr. Harold Bates once ran. A few old, rusty gas pumps stood like sentinels out front. The peeling paint on the building and the creaking sign overhead showed signs of neglect.

We had never done anything like this before. "Alright, remember, we're just two regular customers," I said, trying to sound confident. "Let's grab some snacks and wait for a chance to talk to him."

Eleanor nodded, and we stepped into the station. The dim fluorescent lights flickered, revealing shelves stocked with various snacks, drinks, and automotive supplies.

Dr. Bates stood behind the counter, busy ringing up a customer's purchase. His appearance was drastically different from when I last saw him on TV two years ago. He was now a plump man in his late fifties, with deep-set eyes that held a tired expression. His hair, once neatly styled, was now unkempt and speckled with gray. He wore a faded blue work shirt with the gas station's logo, and his hands were stained with grease from working at the gas station.

We split up and began browsing the shelves, each grabbing a couple of bags of snacks to maintain our cover.

"How should we approach him?" Eleanor asked.

"I think we should start with some small talk," I suggested, glancing over at Dr. Bates. "Maybe ask about the gas station and how long he's been running it. Then we can steer the conversation toward Alice and see how he reacts."

"Okay, sounds like a plan. Let's just hope he doesn't see through us."

We continued to pretend-shop, waiting for the other customers to leave. Slowly, the gas station emptied, and soon it was just us and Dr. Bates. This was our chance.

We approached the counter together, setting our snacks down. Dr. Bates barely glanced up as he scanned the items.

"Afternoon," I said, trying to sound casual. "Busy day?"

He shrugged, still not looking at us. "Just another day. Anything else for you two?"

"Actually, I was curious," I began, leaning slightly on the counter. "How long have you been running this gas station? I remember hearing about your veterinary clinic a couple of years back."

That got his attention. He looked up, his eyes narrowing slightly. "Been running this place for about a year now. Had to close the clinic after… well, some complications."

"I see," I said, nodding. "It must have been a tough transition. Do you miss working with animals?"

Dr. Bates's expression softened just a bit. "Yeah, I do. But life throws curveballs, and you got to roll with it."

Eleanor chimed in. "Do you remember Alice Monroe? She was a friend of ours."

The change in Dr. Bates's demeanor was immediate. His face hardened, and he straightened up, crossing his arms over his chest. "Alice Monroe? Yeah, I remember her. She's the one who got my clinic shut down."

"Alice was found dead in Riverside Park a few days ago," I said, watching his reaction closely. "The circumstances are suspicious, and we're trying to help the police to figure out what happened."

Dr. Bates's eyes flickered with something I couldn't quite place—was it surprise, guilt, or just a well-practiced indifference? "I'm sorry to hear that," he said. "I don't see what that has to do with me."

"Alice exposed the malpractice at your clinic," Eleanor interjected. "We have reason to believe someone who held a resentment against her could be responsible for her death, someone with access to animal tranquilizers."

Dr. Bates's lips curled into a bitter smile. "You think I killed her? I lost everything because of that woman, but I'm not a murderer. I've moved on, as you can see," he said, gesturing to the rundown gas station around him.

"We're just trying to understand if there's any connection," I said, keeping my voice calm. "Did you have any contact with Alice recently? Any confrontations?"

"No," he replied sharply. "I haven't seen or spoken to her since the trial. Look, I understand why you're here, but you're barking up the wrong tree. I'm just trying to get by, running this place. I'm done with that part of my life."

"Dr. Bates, one more thing," I said, stepping closer to the counter. "Where were you on the morning of June 18th, the day Alice died?"

He raised an eyebrow, clearly not expecting the question but unfazed by it. "June 18th? I was here, working at the gas station."

I narrowed my eyes, searching his face for any hint of deceit. "Do you have anyone who can verify that?"

He sighed, his patience wearing thin, but he nodded. "Yes, actually. My assistant, Carol, was here with me all morning. We were doing inventory and dealing with a delivery that came in around 10 AM. She can vouch for me."

"Can we talk to Carol? Just to confirm your alibi?" Eleanor asked.

Dr. Bates shrugged, pulling out his phone. "Sure, if it'll make you believe me." He dialed a number and waited a moment. "Carol, can you come up to the front for a moment?"

A minute later, a woman in her mid-forties with short, curly hair and a warm smile appeared from the back room. "What's up, Dr. Bates?"

"Carol, these ladies have some questions for you. They want to know where I was on the morning of June 18th."

Carol looked puzzled. "You were here, of course. We were doing inventory and then the delivery came in. Why do you ask?"

Eleanor and I exchanged a glance, reading the sincerity in Carol's eyes. "Thank you, Carol," I said.

Dr. Bates leaned against the counter, crossing his arms. "Satisfied? I may have lost my clinic and my reputation, but I'm not a killer."

"Thank you for taking the time to speak with us, Dr. Bates," Eleanor said. "We're just trying to find out what happened to our friend."

Dr. Bates's expression softened slightly. "I hope you find the answers you're looking for. But it wasn't me."

I paid for the snacks and we headed back to the car. Dr. Bates's alibi was solid, and it seemed we had hit a dead end.

"Now what?" Eleanor asked.

"We keep looking."

Chapter 12

The walk from my bookstore to the Athens Chronicle office was short. Today, I hoped to gather some information that could shed light on Alice's death.

The newspaper office was busy with activities when I arrived, the clatter of keyboards and the murmur of conversations filling the air. I asked the receptionist for Penelope Green, and after a brief wait, she appeared from around the corner.

Penelope was a short, slender woman with a sharp, almost angular face. Her dark hair was styled perfectly in a sleek bob that framed her face, and her makeup was applied with precision. She wore a tailored blazer over a crisp blouse, exuding confidence. It was her eyes that drew me in—they were icy and calculating.

"Emma, what brings you here?"

"Penelope, I need to talk to you about Alice."

She arched an eyebrow. "About Alice? What's on your mind?"

We stepped into a small conference room off to the side. As the door closed behind us, I took a deep breath, gathering my thoughts.

"Alice's death wasn't an accident," I began, watching for any reaction. "She was murdered, and we're trying to find out who did it."

Penelope's eyes narrowed. "And you think I know something about it?"

"I know you two had your differences," I replied carefully. "I'm just trying to understand what happened. Did you notice anything unusual in the days leading up to her death? Did Alice mention anyone who might have had a grudge against her?"

Penelope leaned back in her chair, her gaze never leaving mine. For a moment, I thought she might stop speaking to me altogether, but then she sighed, a hint of sadness flickering across her face. "Alice and I were rivals, yes. We competed for stories, for recognition. But that's the nature of this job. It wasn't personal."

"Did she ever mention feeling threatened or being followed?"

Penelope shook her head. "No, she didn't. She was focused on her work, as always. If she was worried about something, she didn't show it. But then again, Alice was good at hiding her true feelings."

There was a moment of silence as I absorbed her words. "One more thing," I said.

"What is it?"

"Where were you on the morning of June 18th?" I asked, watching her closely for any sign of hesitation.

Penelope's eyes widened. "You can't seriously think I had anything to do with her death."

"Just covering all the bases," I replied evenly.

"Fine. I was here at the office, working on a deadline. You can check with the editor, Mr. Thompson. He saw me here, and so did half the staff. I didn't leave the office until well after lunch."

I nodded, taking in her words. "When was the last time you had any contact with Alice?"

"The last time I saw her was a few days before, when we had a meeting about our assignments. After that, she kept to herself. I figured she was busy with her latest story."

"I hope you don't mind me poking around," I said, genuinely appreciative of her cooperation.

"I understand, Emma. I hope you find out what happened to her. Despite everything, Alice didn't deserve this. I envy her for having a wonderful friend like you."

Just as I was about to leave the building, Penelope called after me. "Emma, wait."

I paused and looked back at her. "What is it?"

"There's someone you probably should look into," Penelope said, stepping closer and lowering her voice. "Raymond Collins. He owns a nightclub close to the airport. Alice did a piece on him a while back, exposing illegal gambling in his club. He got arrested because of it."

My brows furrowed in confusion. "I hadn't heard about that story. Why wasn't it bigger news?"

Penelope glanced around as if to make sure no one was eavesdropping. "The newspaper kept it low profile because of an ongoing criminal investigation. The police wanted to avoid tipping off his associates and causing more trouble. It was a high-stakes situation."

"Raymond Collins, what else can you tell me about him?"

"He's dangerous, Emma," Penelope warned. "He's got connections. Alice was brave—or maybe reckless—to go after him. She knew the risks but did it anyway because she believed in exposing the truth."

"Do you think he could be involved in Alice's death?"

Penelope hesitated, then nodded slowly. "It's possible. He would have had motive; Alice's report nearly destroyed his operation. And from what I've heard, he holds grudges."

"Thank you for telling me this, Penelope."

"Watch your back, Emma. Raymond Collins is ruthless."

Chapter 13

Back in the bookstore, I took a deep breath and picked up the phone to call Wyatt, knowing I was about to ask him to bend the rules for me.

"Emma, what's going on?"

"I need your help. I found out something about Alice's case. She did a piece on a guy named Raymond Collins. He owns a nightclub close to the airport and got arrested because of her report on illegal gambling. I think Raymond Collins might be involved in her death."

There was a pause. "Emma, you know I can't get involved in Brown's case. It's his investigation."

I expected this response but wasn't deterred. "Wyatt, Raymond Collins is dangerous. Penelope Green warned me to be careful. But I have to check this out, and I need your help. If you don't come with me, I'll go alone."

The silence on the other end stretched. Finally, Wyatt sighed heavily. "Emma, you can't go there alone. Collins is bad news. Alright, I'll come with you. But we have to keep this low-key."

"When will you have time?"

"I'll pick you up at your house tonight at nine. And Emma, no stunts. We go in, talk, and get out. Got it?"

"Got it. See you then."

***

At exactly nine o'clock, Wyatt's car pulled up in front of my house. As I got into the passenger seat, Wyatt gave me a serious look. "Are you sure you want to go?"

"Absolutely," I replied.

We drove through the dimly lit streets, and the nightclub came into view, its neon sign glowing against the dark sky. Wyatt parked the car and we sat for a moment.

"Remember," Wyatt said, turning to me, "we're just here to talk. No confrontations, no heroics. Got it?"

"Got it," I said.

The music thumped from inside as we walked up to the entrance, the heavy bass vibrating through the pavement. Wyatt exchanged a few words with the bouncer, flashing his badge discreetly, and we were allowed inside.

Inside the nightclub, the air was heavy with the mingling scents of sweat, alcohol, and luxurious cologne. Strobe lights flickered in a mesmerizing pattern, illuminating the crowded dance floor with vibrant hues. Wyatt and I maneuvered through the crowd, making our way toward the bar. The walls were adorned with dark, opulent drapes and neon signs. Mirrors lined one side, reflecting the chaotic energy of the room back at itself, making the club feel even more alive.

Wyatt caught the eye of a passing waitress, a young woman with bright red hair and a tray of drinks balanced effortlessly on one hand. "Excuse me," he said, leaning in close so she could hear him over the music. "We're looking for Raymond Collins. Can you tell us where he is?"

The waitress's eyes flicked to Wyatt's badge, and she nodded quickly. "Follow me."

We followed her through the throng, wound our way past a sleek bar, and into a hallway at the back of the club. The waitress stopped in front of a heavy wooden door and knocked. After a moment, it opened to reveal a burly man with a suspicious glare. The waitress whispered something to him, and he nodded, stepping aside to let us through.

The walls in Raymond Collins's office were dark, lined with shelves holding various trinkets. Raymond Collins sat behind a large, polished mahogany desk. He was a hulking figure, with broad shoulders and an air of menace. His skin was a canvas of tattoos, intricate designs that wound up his neck and across his arms. His piercing eyes instantly sized us up.

"Who the hell are you?"

Wyatt stepped forward, flashing his badge. "Detective Wyatt Miller, APD. This is Emma Wilson, a friend of Alice Monroe."

Raymond's eyes narrowed, a flicker of recognition crossing his face at Alice's name. He leaned back in his chair, regarding us with a mixture of curiosity and suspicion. "Alice Monroe, huh? What do you want with me?"

"Mr. Collins, we need to ask you a few questions about Alice Monroe," I said.

Raymond's fingers drummed on the armrest as he looked at us. "So, Alice Monroe," he said, his voice dripping with sarcasm. "I suppose you're here because you think I had something to do with her death."

"Alice's report on your illegal gambling operation put you in prison for two years. We need to know where you were on the morning of June 18th, when Alice died," I said.

Raymond's eyes flickered with something—resentment, perhaps—but he didn't flinch. "Alice Monroe ruined my life," he said bluntly. "But I didn't kill her. I was out of town that morning, in Atlanta. I was meeting with a business associate, and I have plenty of people who can confirm my alibi."

"Can you provide names and contact information for these people?" Wyatt asked.

Raymond scoffed. "Of course. I was with Anthony Russo, the owner of the biggest club in Atlanta. You can check with him. We had meetings all morning, and there are plenty of witnesses who saw me there."

Wyatt nodded, pulling out his notebook and pen. "We'll follow up on that. But if we find out you're lying—"

"I'm not," Raymond interrupted. "I had no reason to kill Alice. She did her damage, and I did my time. I have a nightclub to run, and I don't want to get into any trouble."

I couldn't help but notice the bitterness that laced his words. "Do you know anyone who might have had a reason to harm her?" I asked.

Raymond paused. "Alice made a lot of enemies," he said slowly. "She was a hell of a reporter, but not everyone appreciated her digging into their business. If you're looking for someone with a grudge, you're going to have a long list."

"Anyone specific come to mind?" Wyatt pressed.

Raymond shook his head. "No one who hated her more than I did. But like I said, I didn't kill her. If anyone did kill her, it would be for the shit she stirred up."

The room fell silent, the weight of his words hanging heavily in the air.

"We'll be in touch if we have more questions," Wyatt said, slipping his notebook back into his pocket.

"Good luck," Raymond said, a trace of sarcasm in his voice. "You'll need it."

The humid night air hit us as we stepped out of the nightclub.

"This is going nowhere," I muttered, kicking a loose pebble on the sidewalk. "Every lead turns into a dead end. Have you made any progress with the animal tranquilizer lead? Have you discovered where those drugs came from?"

"No, we haven't made any progress on that front," Wyatt replied. "Emma, investigating a murder is never easy. We're just getting started and these cases can take time. Going forward, I do not want you to conduct any interviews on your own. Either Daniel or I need to accompany you."

"I can take care of myself, Wyatt."

"I know you can. But people like Raymond Collins are dangerous, and there may be others who are even worse."

"Okay, I'll make sure someone's with me."

Chapter 14

I settled into my chair in the office. This corner of the bookstore was my personal retreat. The sturdy hardwood desk was cluttered with neatly stacked paperwork, a sleek laptop, and a pot of blue orchids.

It was almost time for our meeting. I had called John and Victoria in to discuss strategies for boosting our summer sales. The door creaked open, and John and Victoria entered.

"Come in, sit down." I gestured to the armchairs across from my desk.

"We need to talk about ways to increase our revenue. The summer months are usually slow, and with the college students left, we need to be proactive," I said.

"I've been thinking about this too. What if we host a series of author readings and signings? We could feature local authors and maybe even some regional ones. It would draw people in and give us a chance to showcase our inventory," John suggested.

"We could also offer special discounts during the events to encourage sales. Maybe a 'buy one, get one half off' deal or a discount on related titles," Victoria added.

"I love those ideas. We could promote the events on social media and through our newsletter to reach a wider audience. I also think we should consider creating a summer reading program for kids. It would give families a reason to visit the store regularly," I said.

Victoria's eyes lit up. "Yes, and we could partner with local schools and libraries to spread the word. We could offer small prizes for kids who read a certain number of books over the summer. It would be a great way to build community engagement and foster a love of reading."

John nodded enthusiastically. "And for the adults, how about a summer book club? We could choose a popular title each month and host discussions in the store. It would give our customers a reason to come back and engage with us and each other."

I smiled. "Let's put together a calendar of events and start planning the logistics. We'll need to coordinate with the authors, create promotional materials, and reach out to our contacts in the community."

"I'll handle the social media promotions and contact the local schools and libraries. We can start with the summer reading program for kids," Victoria volunteered.

"I'll reach out to the authors and see who's available for readings and signings. I'll also start organizing the book club details," John said.

"Sounds great. I'm confident that with these initiatives, we'll see a boost in sales and bring more people into our bookstore," I said. "There's something else I need to discuss."

They both looked at me, sensing the seriousness in my tone.

"I'm going to be spending some time investigating Alice's death. That means I'll be in and out of the store more than usual. John, I need you to step up and handle things when I'm not here."

John gave me a reassuring smile. "No problem, Emma. I've got it covered. You focus on what you need to do."

I turned to Victoria. "And Victoria, I know you're already juggling a lot, but any extra help you can provide would be appreciated."

"Absolutely, Emma. I'll do my best to keep everything running smoothly."

"I know I can count on you and hope you understand my situation," I said.

"We completely understand, boss," Victoria said, glancing at John before meeting my gaze again.

***

The moment I stepped into the daycare, the joyful sounds of children playing surrounded me. The rainbow-colored drawings adorning the walls and the energy in the room never failed to brighten my mood. I spotted Oliver's teacher, Mrs. Davis, near the play area, and she waved me over with a smile.

"Hi, Emma," Mrs. Davis greeted me. "Oliver's just finishing up his snack. He's been a busy little bee today."

I smiled, glancing toward the snack table where Oliver sat. He looked up and saw me. "Mommy!"

I crouched down to his level as he ran into my arms. "Hi, little man. Did you have a good day?"

Mrs. Davis approached us, her expression turning a bit serious. "Emma, there's something we need to discuss. Oliver had a bit of a rough patch today. He had a fight with a classmate over a toy, and we had to give him a timeout."

I looked at Oliver, who was now gazing at the floor. "Is that true, Ollie? Did you have a fight?"

He nodded slowly, still not meeting my eyes. "I wanted the truck, but Tommy wouldn't give it to me."

I glanced back at Mrs. Davis. "It happens," she said. "They're still learning how to share."

"We'll talk about this at home," I said, standing up and taking Oliver's hand.

As we walked to the car, I squeezed Oliver's hand gently. "Ollie, do you know why it's important to share with your friends?"

He looked up at me. "Why, Mommy?"

"Because sharing is a way to show kindness," I explained. "When we share, we make our friends happy. Wouldn't you want Tommy to share with you if you wanted to play with something?"

Oliver nodded. "Yes, Mommy."

I kissed his forehead. "Next time, let's ask nicely and take turns, okay? It's important to be kind."

"Okay, Mommy," he said, a small smile creeping onto his face.

As I stepped outside the daycare with Oliver's hand in mine, I almost collided with a tall, lean figure. I looked up to see Jack, Alice's ex-boyfriend, standing before me with a surprised look on his face. Jack had always been quite the sight, with his defined jawline, tousled dark locks, and piercing emerald eyes. He was dressed casually in a fitting t-shirt and khaki shorts, carrying a laptop bag over his shoulder that gave off a tech-savvy vibe.

"Emma, I didn't expect to see you here."

"Jack, what are you doing here?"

"I'm picking up my niece. My sister's running late."

Oliver tugged at my hand, and I smiled at him before turning back to Jack. "I've been meaning to talk to you. Do you have a moment?"

"Sure, what's up?"

"It's about Alice. You've probably heard she's... gone. I'm trying to find out what happened to her."

A flicker of pain crossed Jack's face. "Yeah, I heard. I'm sorry, Emma."

"I need to know if you have any information, anything at all that might help. Where were you the morning she died?"

Jack sighed. "I was at work. My boss and several coworkers can vouch for me. We were in meetings all morning, and I didn't leave the office until late in the afternoon."

I studied his face, but he seemed sincere. "Can I ask what really happened between you two?"

"Alice and I had our differences. She was driven, always chasing the next big story. It created a distance between us. Despite our messy breakup, I never wished her any harm, Emma. But there's something else you should know."

"What is it?"

"Alice was having an affair with Samuel Lewis, the manager of the Georgian Grand Hotel."

My heart skipped a beat. "What? Are you sure?"

"Yeah, I'm sure. I found out shortly before we broke up. It's one of the reasons we ended things. Samuel's married. His wife, Chloe... she's not someone to mess with."

Alice had never mentioned Samuel Lewis to me, let alone an affair. "Why didn't she tell me?" I muttered, more to myself than to Jack.

"Alice was colorful. However, just so you are aware, Chloe might have found out about the affair. Chloe is fiercely protective of her family and their reputation. If she knew about the affair, she could have had a motive to..."

He didn't finish the sentence, but the implication hung heavily in the air. "You think Chloe Lewis killed Alice?" I asked.

"It's a possibility. Take care, Emma. I have to go now."

As he walked away, I stood there, gripping Oliver's hand. The revelation about Alice's affair with Samuel Lewis felt like a bombshell. I buckled Oliver into his car seat, my mind racing with questions. If Jack was right, and Chloe had found out about the affair, she could indeed have a motive for murder.

Chapter 15

The sun painted our backyard in a shade of gold as Daniel and I bustled around, making the final preparations for our July 4th barbecue party. The scent of freshly cut grass mingled with the mouthwatering aroma of the grill, where Daniel was busy flipping burgers and turning ears of corn.

"How's it going over there?" I called to him as I spread a red-and-white checkered tablecloth over the picnic table.

"Drinks are on ice, and the first batch of burgers will be done soon," Daniel replied, glancing up with a smile. He gestured to the ice cooler he had filled with beer and wine, now nestled in the shade.

"Perfect. I'm just about done with the chicken pasta salad. How's Oliver doing?"

Oliver was toddling around the yard with an air of serious concentration, carrying plastic cups from one side of the table to the other. "He's been a big help," Daniel said with a chuckle. "I think he's set the record for most cups moved in a single afternoon."

I smiled, watching Oliver's earnest little face as he placed another cup on the table. "Good job, my little man!" I praised him, earning a beaming smile in return.

I grabbed the large bowl of chicken pasta salad from the kitchen counter and brought it outside, placing it in the center of the table. Next, I arranged a platter of salsa and chips. The backyard looked festive, with colorful streamers hanging from the trees and small American flags stuck into the flower beds.

"Think we're ready?" I asked Daniel.

"I'd say so. Just in time, too—I think I hear a car pulling up."

Sure enough, the sound of tires crunching on the driveway signaled the arrival of our first guests. I saw Benjamin walking through the gate, carrying a large tray covered with foil.

"Hey, Benjamin!" I called out. "What've you got there?"

He grinned, lifting the tray slightly. "BBQ baby back ribs. Thought I'd contribute something extra tasty."

I walked over to him, the mouthwatering smell of the ribs reaching me through the foil. "Wow, these smell good!"

"Taste good too. Family recipe."

As we were setting the tray on the table, I saw Eleanor arrive, balancing a chocolate cake in her hands. I hurried over to help her. "Eleanor, that looks incredible! Need a hand?"

"I've got it. I brought something sweet."

Benjamin stepped forward, his eyes twinkling with mischief. "Hi, I'm Benjamin. That's an impressive cake you've got there. Did you make it, or did you have to wrestle it from a bakery?"

Eleanor chuckled, setting the cake down on the dessert table. "Nice to meet you, Benjamin. My name is Eleanor and I baked it myself. What did you bring to this feast?"

"BBQ baby back ribs," Benjamin replied, lifting the foil to reveal the glistening ribs. "I promise they taste as good as they look."

Eleanor's eyes lit up. "Those look fantastic. I might have to steal a few before the others get their hands on them."

Benjamin laughed, his eyes never leaving Eleanor's. "You're welcome to as many as you want. Maybe you can share a slice of that cake in return?"

Eleanor smiled. "Deal."

As they continued to chat, I couldn't help but notice the easy chemistry between them.

Just then, Avery and her husband Jimmy walked in through the gate. Avery held a bottle of wine in one hand.

"Avery, Jimmy! So glad you could make it!" I called out.

Avery handed me the bottle of wine. "Happy to be here, Emma."

Jimmy nodded in agreement. "Yeah, everything smells incredible." He turned to Daniel, who was manning the grill. "Hey, Daniel, when are we hitting the golf course? I've been itching to play."

"Whenever you're ready, Jimmy. I've got plenty of time now that it's summer break. Just say the word."

As they started talking golf, I noticed John, Victoria, and the twin sisters Sophia and Evelyn arriving together. John carried a basket of juicy Georgia peaches. The sight of the bright, fresh fruit brought a smile to my face.

"John, Victoria, Sophia, and Evelyn! You guys brought peaches!"

John grinned, holding up the basket. "Can't have a summer barbecue without some Georgia peaches, right?"

Victoria's eyes scanned the yard with delight. "Nice party, Emma."

Sophia and Evelyn chimed in together. "Happy Independence Day!"

Daniel came over, wiping his hands on a towel. "Hey everyone, glad you could make it. Those peaches look perfect. We'll have to make sure they get a prime spot on the dessert table."

I ushered them toward the growing buffet of food. The backyard was now buzzing with conversation and laughter.

I turned my attention back to the table, arranging the food and making sure everything was in order. Daniel gave me a thumbs-up, clearly pleased with how the party was going. I saw Benjamin and Eleanor still deep in conversation, their plates now empty but their smiles wide.

"Looks like they're hitting it off." Daniel came up beside me and wrapped an arm around my shoulders.

"Yeah," I agreed, leaning into him. "I think they are."

Everyone clustered around the table or settled into lawn chairs out in the yard. Avery and Jimmy were chatting with John and Victoria, while Sophia and Evelyn entertained Oliver with their twin antics.

As the sun dipped lower, I spotted Wyatt, Susan, and their two boys, Noah and James, making their way through the gate. Susan carried a large tray of grilled salmon, the delicious aroma wafting through the air. I walked over to greet them.

"Susan! Wyatt! Welcome!" I exclaimed, hugging Susan warmly. "You brought salmon! It smells amazing."

Susan returned the hug. "We wouldn't miss it for the world, Emma. I thought the salmon would be a nice addition to all the delicious food you have here."

I turned to Noah and James, ruffling their hair. "Hey there, you two! Ready to have some fun?"

Noah, the older of the two, grinned. "Yeah, Aunt Emma! Can we play with Oliver?"

"Of course! He's been waiting for you."

Just then, Daniel walked over with Oliver in his arms. "Hey, Wyatt, Susan," he greeted them, setting Oliver down. "Glad you could make it."

Oliver immediately ran over to his cousins. "Noah! James! Let's play! My dad bought me a brand new bike," he squealed, leading them toward the yard where a few toys and games were already set up.

"Here's your favorite, brother." Daniel handed Wyatt a cold beer, clinking their bottles together in a toast.

Wyatt took a sip, nodding appreciatively. "Thanks, Daniel. Your parties are always top-notch, Emma."

I smiled, feeling a warm sense of pride. "It's wonderful having everyone here."

Susan placed the tray of salmon on the table, adding to the already impressive spread. "This all looks incredible. Did you make the chicken pasta salad, Emma?"

"I did." I handed plates to Susan and Wyatt. "You should try Benjamin's BBQ baby back ribs as well."

"Great idea." Susan loaded her plate with chicken pasta salad and a rib.

Daniel went back to manning the grill, carefully flipping burgers and checking on the corn on the cob.

"Wyatt, you've got to try Daniel's burger," I said. "He put a lot of effort into perfecting his recipe this year."

Wyatt grinned, his eyes lighting up with amusement. "Well, if it's as good as you say, I'd better not miss out." He turned to Daniel and called out, "Save one of those masterpieces for me, will you?"

Daniel chuckled, giving Wyatt a thumbs-up. "Coming right up!"

As Wyatt headed toward the grill to assemble his burger, Susan turned to me. "Emma, since you and Daniel are hosting the July 4th party, we thought it would be nice if Wyatt and I hosted the family Thanksgiving this year. What do you think?"

"That sounds wonderful, Susan. I'd love that. It's been a while since we all gathered at your place for Thanksgiving."

"Perfect! We'll start planning soon. I want this Thanksgiving to be special."

Just then, Wyatt returned, holding a perfectly assembled burger. He took a bite and his eyes widened in appreciation. "Emma, you weren't kidding. This is fantastic!"

"I told you! He's been experimenting with different spices and grilling techniques."

"He's got a real talent for cooking beef."

I glanced around the backyard. Oliver was running around with his cousins, his laughter ringing out joyfully. "We cut down several big pine trees to give Oliver more room to play in the backyard," I said, turning back to Wyatt and Susan. "It's made a huge difference. He loves having more space to run around."

Susan looked over at Oliver. "Kids need room to play and move around."

Wyatt chimed in with a nod, "The yard looks fantastic now. And we have more space for the fireworks later tonight."

As Susan went to retrieve a bottle of water, Wyatt leaned in close to me and whispered, "Emma, we've found something interesting and maybe related to Alice's case. But you have to keep this information confidential."

"Of course, I won't tell anyone," I replied eagerly.

"A couple of months ago, someone stole multiple bottles of animal tranquilizers from the Athens Zoo."

I frowned, trying to make sense of the information. "How did that happen?"

"There was a break-in at the zoo's veterinary storage. The security footage was tampered with, so they don't have a clear image of the thief. It was all very professionally done."

"Have you caught the person who did it?"

"We're still investigating. However, just because the tranquilizers were stolen doesn't necessarily mean they were used on Alice," Wyatt said.

"Do you have any leads on who might have stolen the tranquilizers?"

"Not solid ones," Wyatt admitted. "But we're looking into anyone with connections to the zoo and veterinary medicine. It's a starting point."

"I am happy to hear that things are moving forward."

As the sun descended below the horizon, the first fireworks illuminated the sky with a myriad of colors. The kids paused in their play, looking up in awe at the display.

Daniel raised his beer in a toast. "Here's to our family and friends. Happy Fourth of July, everyone!"

We all raised our glasses, echoing his sentiments. "Happy Fourth of July!"

As the night settled in and the sky turned a deep indigo, Daniel appeared with a large box of fireworks, his face alight with excitement. The crowd in our backyard gathered around, eager for the show to begin.

"Noah, James, come over here," Daniel called, gesturing to the boys. "You guys want to help light these up?"

The boys' eyes widened with excitement, and they rushed over. Daniel handed each of them a firework, showing them how to light the fuses.

"Remember, always stand back after you light it. And make sure you're not too close."

One by one, Noah and James took turns lighting the fireworks. The rockets shot into the sky, bursting into brilliant colors. The crowd oohed and aahed, the sound of laughter and cheers filling the night air.

Daniel knelt beside Oliver, who was watching his cousins with wide-eyed wonder. "Okay, buddy," Daniel said softly, holding a sparkler in his hand. "Do you want to try lighting one?"

Oliver nodded eagerly, his little hands reaching for the sparkler. Daniel guided him, helping him hold the lighter and igniting the sparkler's tip. As the sparks flew, Oliver's face lit up with pure delight.

"Look, Mommy!" he squealed, waving the sparkler around.

"You're doing great, Ollie!" I called back.

More fireworks soared into the sky, painting it with dazzling displays of light and color. The brilliant bursts of reds, blues, and golds reflected in the faces of our friends and family.

Standing there, I felt a bittersweet pang in my heart. I glanced up at the sky, the fireworks bursting like stars against the darkness. I couldn't help but think of Alice. It was as if she were looking down at us, sharing this beautiful moment with us.

Chapter 16

I was in the middle of reorganizing the history section at the bookstore when the phone rang. It was mid-afternoon and there were not many customers in sight.

"Emma's Haven, how can I help you?" I answered.

There was a brief pause before a male voice spoke, low and cautious. "Is this Emma Wilson?"

"Yes, this is she. Who's calling?"

"You don't know me, but my name is Sam. I'm an environmental activist, and I was close to Alice Monroe."

I froze, the book I was holding slipping from my grasp and thudding softly onto the floor. "Alice Monroe? How did you know her?"

"We worked together on several projects. Alice was about to expose a major environmental scandal before she died. It involves Gregory Hale's construction company illegally dumping toxic waste into the river."

The words hit me like a punch to the gut. Gregory Hale was a well-known businessman in Athens, celebrated for his philanthropy and success. A few days ago, Benjamin mentioned that Gregory had recently made a $50,000 donation to the University. The idea that he could be involved in something so sinister was almost too much to process. "Are you sure? Gregory Hale? That's a serious accusation."

"I'm positive. Alice had gathered substantial evidence. She was about to go public with it, but then... well, you know what happened."

My mind raced. "Do you have any of the evidence Alice collected?"

"No, she kept it well hidden."

"Can we meet, Sam?"

"No. It's not convenient for me to meet you. I've got to go." He ended the call in a hurry.

After the unsettling phone call from Sam, I sat behind the counter, my mind racing with the implications of what I'd just learned. With trembling fingers, I dialed Daniel's number.

"Hey, babe. How's everything at the bookstore?"

"Dan, I need to tell you something. A man by the name of Sam called me and claimed to be an environmental activist who knew Alice."

There was a pause on the other end of the line. "Okay… What else did he say?"

"He told me that before Alice died, she was on the verge of exposing a major environmental scandal. Gregory Hale's construction company has been illegally dumping toxic waste into the river."

There was a stunned silence. "Gregory Hale?" Daniel finally said. "Emma, that's a serious allegation. Gregory is an alumnus of the University and he has been seen as a pillar of the town."

"I know. But Sam was adamant. He said Alice had gathered substantial evidence. This could be a motive for murder."

I could hear Daniel rubbing his temples the way he always did when he was deep in thought. "If this is true, it changes everything. But we need to be sure," Daniel said.

"Do you think it's possible that Gregory ambushed Alice with an animal tranquilizer gun and caused her to drown?"

"It's possible," Daniel admitted, though I could hear the reluctance in his voice. "If he felt threatened by what Alice had uncovered, he might have taken drastic measures to protect himself and his company. We need evidence, babe. Solid evidence. Is it possible for us to have a conversation with this Sam and gather further details?"

"I asked him earlier for contact information, but he refused to give me any."

"Babe, we need to take this with a grain of salt. Anonymous calls can be tricky. There's no way to verify the information right now."

"I also thought the call was kind of weird, but I don't have many leads to follow right now."

"Just be open-minded. Let's not jump to conclusions without more evidence."

"There's something else too. Jack, Alice's ex-boyfriend, told me that Alice was having an affair with Samuel Lewis.

Jack thinks that Chloe, Samuel's wife, might have killed Alice out of jealousy," I said.

"Samuel Lewis? The hotel manager?"

"Yes."

Daniel was silent for a moment. "That's a lot to take in. If Chloe found out about the affair, she could have a motive."

"I can't believe Alice didn't tell me about the affair. We were best friends. We told each other everything."

Daniel's tone softened. "Emma, there could be a lot of reasons why Alice didn't tell you. Maybe she was ashamed or felt guilty about it."

"But why? We always shared our problems and our secrets. Why keep this from me?"

"Babe, sometimes people keep secrets because they're trying to deal with their own emotions. Maybe Alice was trying to figure things out on her own before she talked to you about it."

I leaned back in my chair, staring at the ceiling. "I suppose. It's just hard to accept that she was dealing with something so significant and didn't feel she could come to me."

"Remember, Alice was human. She made mistakes and had her struggles. Maybe she didn't tell you because she was afraid of losing your respect."

"I never would have judged her, Dan. I loved her like a sister."

"And she knew that," Daniel said firmly. "But sometimes, the fear of disappointing someone we care about can be overwhelming. It can make us do things that seem out of character."

"You're right. I need to remember that."

Chapter 17

My heart thumped nervously when I arrived at Gregory Hale's construction company. The modern office building was an impressive sight, all sleek glass and steel, standing tall against the blue sky. When I walked through the revolving doors, I was greeted by the cool, sterile air of the lobby.

The lobby was spacious, with polished marble floors and a large reception desk sat at the center, staffed by a young woman who smiled professionally.

"Hello, I'm an environmental activist," I began. "I'd like to speak with your manager about the company's environmental policies."

"One moment, please," the receptionist acknowledged with a nod before making a brief phone call. Within moments, a short, well-dressed man arrived. He had a pleasant attitude, with sleek dark hair and a pair of glasses that added to his intellectual appearance. He held out his hand for me to shake.

"Good morning, I'm Lucas Scott. I'm one of the managers here. How can I help you?"

I shook his hand. "Good morning, Mr. Scott. My name is Emma Wilson. I'm with Green Horizons Initiative, and we're very interested in learning more about your company's environmental practices. Would you have some time to discuss this?" Alice had been a member of Green Horizons Initiative, an environmental organization. I was there on her behalf.

"Of course, Emma. Why don't we step into the conference room?"

Lucas led me through the open-plan office space. It was meticulously designed, with glass-walled meeting rooms and collaborative workspaces. Employees sat at ergonomic desks, typing away on computers, the hum of productivity filling the air.

We reached a conference room at the end of the hall. Lucas opened the glass door and gestured for me to enter. The room was spacious, with floor-to-ceiling windows that offered a panoramic view of Athens. A long, polished wooden table occupied the center, surrounded by high-backed leather chairs. A large screen was mounted on one wall, and a few potted plants added a touch of greenery to the otherwise minimalist decor.

"Please, have a seat." Lucas motioned to one of the chairs. "Can I get you anything? Water, coffee?"

"I'm fine, thank you." I sat down and placed my bag on the table.

Lucas took a seat across from me. "So, Emma, what specifically would you like to discuss regarding our environmental policies?"

"We've heard some concerns from the community about potential environmental impacts related to your company's operations. Specifically, there have been rumors about improper waste disposal practices. As an activist group, we're very interested in ensuring that all companies adhere to the highest environmental standards."

"Of course. As a large construction company, we generate a significant amount of waste every day. It's a major responsibility, and we take it very seriously."

Lucas maintained his polite demeanor, though I noticed a flicker of something in his eyes—panic, perhaps, or caution. "We deal with several types of waste: construction debris, hazardous materials, and everyday operational waste. For construction debris, we have a rigorous recycling program. Materials like concrete, wood, and metal are sorted and sent to recycling facilities."

I nodded, jotting down notes. "And what about hazardous materials?"

"We handle those with extreme caution," Lucas continued. "We have specialized containment and disposal protocols to ensure that hazardous waste doesn't contaminate the environment. This includes things like asbestos, lead-based paints, and certain chemicals used in construction."

"And operational waste?" I asked.

"Operational waste is handled much like it would be in any large office. We have extensive recycling programs for paper, plastic, and electronics. We also encourage our employees to minimize waste through various sustainability initiatives."

I raised an eyebrow. "That sounds comprehensive. How does your company ensure compliance with environmental regulations?"

"We allocate a significant portion of our budget to waste management and environmental compliance. We work with environmental consultants and regularly conduct audits to make sure we're adhering to all local, state, and federal regulations. It's a substantial investment, but we believe it's essential for the long-term health of our community and the environment."

I was impressed by the commitment of the company. "Do you have any specific initiatives or programs you're particularly proud of?"

"Absolutely. One of our flagship programs is our green building initiative. We focus on using sustainable materials and energy-efficient designs in our projects. We've also partnered with local environmental organizations to support conservation efforts and community clean-up projects."

I felt a mix of admiration and suspicion. "With such a large operation, mistakes and oversights can happen. How does your company handle any potential issues that arise?"

"Transparency is key. If any issues are identified, we address them immediately and transparently. We believe in being accountable to the public and our stakeholders. It's important for us to maintain trust and demonstrate our commitment to environmental stewardship."

My heart was pounding in my chest, but I knew I had to press on. "It all sounds very impressive, Mr. Scott. But I have to ask—has your company engaged in any illegal dumping of toxic waste into the river?"

Lucas's expression didn't change, but I noticed a slight tightening around his eyes. "Absolutely not," he said firmly. "Our company follows all environmental laws and regulations to the letter. We would never risk the health of our community or the environment."

I maintained eye contact, trying to gauge his sincerity. "I understand your position, but there have been rumors and concerns from the community. I'm just trying to get to the truth."

Lucas leaned forward slightly, his tone becoming more insistent. "Emma, I assure you, there is no illegal dumping from our company. These concerns are completely unfounded. I suggest you stop this baseless investigation before it causes unnecessary harm to our reputation and the community's trust."

I took a deep breath, deciding to change my approach. "Do you know Alice Monroe?" I asked, watching him closely.

"No, I've never heard that name before. Should I have?"

I studied his face, searching for any sign of deception, but his expression remained neutral and unreadable. "She was a journalist who was investigating environmental issues in the area. She recently passed away under suspicious circumstances."

Lucas's brow furrowed slightly, but he didn't seem perturbed. "I'm sorry to hear that, but as I said, I've never heard of her. If there's anything else you need, please let me know. Otherwise, I'd appreciate it if you could conclude your visit."

"Thank you for your time, Mr. Scott."

He stood up and extended his hand again. "It was my pleasure."

I shook his hand and left the conference room. As I walked through the sleek office and out into the hot afternoon air, I couldn't shake the feeling that I was missing something. Lucas had been polite and professional, but there was an underlying tension in our conversation that I couldn't ignore. If Gregory Hale's construction company was involved in illegal dumping, they were doing a masterful job of covering it up.

Chapter 18

Avery and I stood side by side on the front porch of Chloe Lewis's house. The house was a charming, well-kept cottage. The neighborhood was quiet, save for the occasional chirping of birds. I rang the doorbell, feeling a knot of nervousness tighten in my stomach. After a brief pause, Chloe appeared at the door. She was a beautiful woman, with voluptuous curves and dark hair pulled back into a tight bun. She looked surprised to see us.

"Mrs. Lewis. I'm Emma Wilson, and this is my friend Avery. We were hoping to speak with you for a few minutes about Alice Monroe."

Chloe's face hardened. "Alice is dead. And you're not the police. I have nothing to say."

"I understand, Mrs. Lewis, but we're trying to help the police find out what happened to Alice. There's a rumor that your husband, Samuel, was having an affair with her before she died."

At the mention of the affair, Chloe's eyes widened, and her expression shifted from irritation to shock. She glanced around quickly, as if to make sure no one was eavesdropping, then stepped aside. "Okay, let's talk inside. But make it quick."

We followed her into the living room, a space tastefully decorated with vintage furniture. She gestured for us to sit on the sofa while she took a seat in an armchair opposite us.

"So, what do you want to know?" Chloe asked, crossing her arms defensively.

"We heard that you confronted Alice at her workplace. Is that true?" I asked, meeting her gaze.

Chloe's jaw tightened, and she looked away for a moment before nodding. "Yes, it's true. I found out about the affair in the worst possible way. I saw a message on Samuel's phone. It was from Alice, asking to meet. At first, I couldn't believe it. Samuel had always been so dedicated to our family."

Chloe sighed and continued. "I confronted Samuel that night. He didn't deny it. He admitted they had a one-night stand, but he swore it was over. He said it had been a mistake, that he loved me and wanted to make things right."

"And what did you do?" I asked softly.

"I was furious, hurt, betrayed," Chloe said, her voice trembling. "I needed to hear Alice's side of the story. So, I went to see her, face-to-face. I was furious. She was destroying my family."

Avery and I exchanged a glance.

"What happened during that confrontation?" Avery asked.

Chloe's eyes filled with anger. "I told her to stay away from my husband. I threatened her and said things I probably shouldn't have. But I was desperate. She had no right to destroy our lives."

"Did she say anything to you?" I asked.

"She tried to defend herself, said it wasn't like that between them. But I didn't believe her. I thought she was lying to cover up the affair."

"How did Alice and Samuel meet?" I pressed.

"At environmental activist events. They both cared about the same causes, and I suppose that drew them together." Chloe's shoulders slumped.

I knew I had to ask the difficult question, even if it risked further upsetting her. "Mrs. Lewis, where were you and your husband the morning of June 18th, when Alice died?"

Her face grew stern instantly. "Why do you want to know? You're not the police."

I took a deep breath, trying to keep my tone calm and steady. "I understand this is difficult, but we're just trying to find the truth about what happened to Alice. Any information could help."

Chloe's eyes flashed with anger. "I've already told you more than I should have. I don't need to justify myself to you. It's time for you to leave."

"Mrs. Lewis, please. We just need to know if—"

"I said leave!" Chloe snapped, her voice rising. "I've had enough of this interrogation. Get out of my house!"

Avery stepped forward, her temper flaring. "You don't have to be so hostile, Mrs. Lewis. We're just trying to—"

Chloe cut her off, pointing toward the door. "I don't care what you're trying to do. Get out, both of you!"

"Come on, Avery," I said, gently tugging her arm. "Let's go."

As we stepped onto the porch, Chloe slammed the door behind us.

We walked to the car in silence, the weight of the encounter hanging heavily over us. Once we were inside, Avery turned to me. "That went well," she muttered sarcastically. "Do you think Chloe could have killed Alice?"

I sighed. "It's possible. She was angry, and she might have been desperate enough to do something drastic."

Avery nodded. "But would she have had the means and opportunity? Would she use an animal tranquilizer and a dart gun? That seems... calculated."

"You're right. It does seem more like something someone with specific knowledge and access would do. But we can't rule out the possibility that Chloe might have known someone who could help her."

"Like Samuel," Avery said quietly. "If he was involved in the affair, he might have had a motive to get rid of Alice too."

"We need to find out more about Samuel's connections and see if there's any link to the animal tranquilizers. And we need to keep an eye on Chloe. Her reaction was... intense. Maybe we can find someone else who can verify their alibi," I said.

"Did you know anything about Alice's affair with Samuel Lewis before Jack told you?" Avery asked.

"No, Alice never mentioned anything about it to me. That's why I was so surprised when Jack broke the news. Our conversation with Chloe today at least confirmed something did happen between Alice and Samuel," I replied.

"Perhaps it was just a brief fling that Alice didn't feel the need to share with us."

"It seems like Chloe is still upset about it."

As I drove away, I couldn't shake the feeling that there was more to Chloe's reaction than just anger. She might be hiding something.

Chapter 19

I arrived at Emma's Haven early that morning. The peaceful quiet of dawn was shattered the moment I turned the corner and saw my beloved bookstore.

All three display windows were shattered, the glass glinting menacingly in the faint morning light. Large rocks lay scattered among the shards. I hurried forward, my footsteps crunching on the broken glass.

The inside of the bookstore was a chaotic mess. Books that had once been neatly arranged in the display were now strewn across the floor, their pages crumpled. A few of my favorite hardcovers lay open, their spines broken, looking as if they had been trampled in the rush.

The display tables had been upended, their contents spilled onto the floor. Small trinkets, which I had carefully selected to complement the books, were scattered everywhere. One of the tables had a deep gouge in its surface where a rock had struck it.

The cash register area was no better. Papers, receipts, and small items that had been on the counter were now a part of the mess on the floor. My carefully arranged collection of bookmarks was now a jumbled pile mixed with glass and debris. The register itself had a dent in its side as if someone had taken a swing at it with one of the rocks.

I took a deep breath, attempting to calm my trembling hands, before dialing the police.

"Athens Police Department, what's your emergency?" the dispatcher answered.

"This is Emma Wilson. My bookstore's windows have been smashed. Please send someone quickly." I gave the dispatcher the address of my bookstore.

"We'll have officers there right away," the dispatcher assured me.

I hung up and began to carefully navigate the mess, checking for anything missing. It didn't seem like anything valuable had been taken; the rare books were still in their locked cabinet. It appeared to be an act of vandalism.

I called up Daniel and he promised to drop off Oliver at daycare and then come over straight away.

Within minutes, two police officers arrived. They introduced themselves as Officer Reynolds and Officer Martinez.

"I'm so sorry this happened, Ms. Wilson. Can you tell us what you found when you arrived?" asked Officer Reynolds, a man in his mid-30s with a kind face.

I tried to keep my voice steady. "I got here and saw the windows broken. Rocks were thrown through them, and the inside is a mess, but it doesn't look like anything valuable was stolen."

Officer Martinez, a petite woman with a no-nonsense demeanor, took notes, glancing around the store. "Do you have any idea who might have done this? Any recent conflicts or threats?"

I hesitated, thinking of the investigation into Alice's death and the people I had been questioning. "I've been asking a lot of questions about my friend Alice Monroe's death. She was a journalist, and I've been following up on her leads. It could be related."

"We'll look into that angle," Officer Martinez said. "In the meantime, we'll collect evidence and see if there are any security cameras nearby that might have caught something."

I nodded, grateful for their help.

As they began their investigation, I stood in the wreckage of my bookstore, feeling a mix of anger and sorrow.

Just then, the door opened, and Daniel rushed in. "Babe!" he called, hurrying over to me. He wrapped his arms around me, pulling me into a tight embrace. "Are you okay?"

I clung to him, my tears finally spilling over. "I don't know, Dan. Who would do this? Why?"

He held me tighter. "We'll find out who did this."

We stood there for a moment, just holding each other. Finally, Daniel pulled back slightly. "You visited Chloe Lewis yesterday, right?"

I wiped my eyes. "Yes, we talked about Samuel's affair with Alice. She seemed upset but...I don't know. Do you think she could have something to do with this?"

Daniel ran a hand through his hair. "It's hard to say. People react in unpredictable ways when they're hurt or angry. Due to the timing of your visit and the vandalization today, it's a possibility we can't ignore."

"Maybe she or someone else felt threatened by what we're uncovering," I said.

Officer Reynolds closed his notebook and gave us a sympathetic smile. "We've documented everything we can for now. We'll file the report and keep you updated on any developments."

"In the meantime, we suggest installing some security cameras if you haven't already. It might help deter any further incidents," Officer Martinez added.

"Thank you both for your help. It means a lot to us," I said.

Officer Reynolds gave me a reassuring nod. "We'll do everything we can to find out who did this. If you remember anything else or notice anything unusual, don't hesitate to contact us."

Daniel extended his hand, shaking theirs firmly. "We appreciate it."

As they turned to leave, Officer Martinez paused at the door. "Take care, Emma."

I watched as they walked out, the bell above the door jingling softly in their wake.

"I can't believe this happened," I said, picking up a ruined book from the floor. "I should have installed security cameras ages ago."

"Don't blame yourself, Emma. No one could have predicted this."

"I should have thought about it. It's not like we're in some crime-free utopia. We have valuable things here, and I should have taken more precautions."

Daniel knelt to help me pick up the scattered books. "Well, there's no use dwelling on it now. The important thing is that we take steps to prevent it from happening again. I'll look up some companies that install security systems. We'll get quotes and find the best one. Do you think the insurance will cover the damage and repair?"

I sighed, leaning against the counter. "I hope so. The store has very good insurance policies, but until I talk to them, I won't know for sure."

"The office of the insurance company should be open by now. Let's call them and hopefully, they'll send someone out to assess the damage," Daniel said.

I pulled the phone out of my pocket and dialed the insurance company's number. After what felt like an eternity, a calm voice came on the line.

"Good morning, this is Sylvia with Grayson Insurance. How can I assist you today?"

"Hi, Sylvia. My name is Emma Wilson. I own the Emma's Haven bookstore in downtown Athens. My bookstore was vandalized last night. All three display windows were broken, and there's significant damage inside," I said, trying to keep my voice steady.

"I'm so sorry to hear that, Ms. Wilson. Let's get some details so we can start processing your claim. Can you tell me exactly what happened?" Sylvia asked.

I recounted the events as clearly as I could. She listened attentively, typing as I spoke. When I finished, there was a brief silence as she reviewed the information.

"Ms. Wilson, given the extent of the damage, we'll need to send an assessor to your location. Can you confirm your address for me?"

I gave her the address, feeling a small glimmer of hope. "How soon can someone be here?"

"Given the urgency, we can have someone there within the next hour," Sylvia assured me. "They will assess the damage and help you with the next steps."

"Thank you, Sylvia," I said. "One more thing—can I start cleaning up the mess, or do I need to wait for the assessor?"

"It's fine to start cleaning up, Ms. Wilson. Just make sure to take some photographs of the damage before you begin, for documentation purposes," she advised.

"I'll do that."

Daniel appeared from the back room, a broom in his hand. "What did they say?"

"They're sending someone over within the hour to assess the damage," I told him. "We can start cleaning up, but we need to take photos first."

"Got it," he said, handing me a broom. "I'll start with the pictures."

As Daniel moved around the store, snapping photos of the broken windows, the scattered books, and the general disarray, I began to sweep up the glass shards. The rhythmic motion of sweeping helped to calm my mind.

Daniel finished taking photos and joined me in the clean-up. We had just finished clearing one corner of the store when a knock on the door startled us both. I looked up to see a man in a neatly pressed white shirt, carrying a clipboard and a camera.

"Ms. Wilson?" he asked, stepping inside. "I'm Tony from Grayson Insurance. I'm here to assess the damage."

"Thank you for coming so quickly, Tony," I said, leading him further into the store. "As you can see, it's quite a mess."

Tony surveyed the scene and took notes. "Let's start with the windows and work our way through. I'll need to take some photos and document everything for the claim."

Daniel and I stood back, letting Tony do his job. My attention was drawn to the sound of voices murmuring outside. I walked to the door and peered out. A group of people had gathered, some just passing by and others from nearby shops.

Mrs. Jenkins from the bakery next door stepped forward. "Emma, dear, what happened? Are you alright?"

I tried to muster a reassuring smile. "I'm okay, Mrs. Jenkins. Just...shaken up. Someone vandalized the store last night."

She shook her head. "This is terrible. If there's anything we can do to help, just let us know. I'm glad the police were here."

"Yes, they will investigate."

Mr. Thompson from the hardware store joined us, his expression grim. "I'll get my guys to help with the cleanup. We can board up those windows until you can get them replaced."

"We will come to your store to buy some hardware to board up the windows," I replied, feeling a swell of gratitude.

After Tony had finished documenting the damage, Daniel and I went back to the store. Before leaving the store, Tony handed me his business card and assured me he would stay in touch.

Armed with brooms and dustpans, Daniel and I began to clean up the shattered glass that littered the floor. I heard the jingle of the doorbell and turned to see John and Victoria enter.

"Emma, what happened?" John asked.

"Someone threw rocks through the windows last night. The police just left. They're going to investigate, but for now, we need to clean up this mess."

Victoria stepped closer. "I'm so sorry, boss. What do you want me to do?"

"First, we'll need to sweep up the broken glass and gather the books off the floor," I said. "John, you and Daniel can board up the windows with plywood. I'll find a glass contractor as soon as possible."

John nodded. "I'll head to the hardware store and get what we need."

As John left, Daniel, Victoria and I began the painstaking process of cleaning up. We worked in silence for a while, the only sounds were the crunch of glass underfoot and the rustle of pages as we picked up the books.

"Be careful not to step on the broken glass on the floor," I warned.

"Be mindful of where you're stepping," Daniel chimed in.

"This is just awful," Victoria said. "Who would do something like this?"

I hesitated, then decided to share my suspicions. "I think it might be related to my investigation of Alice's death. I've made some people nervous. This could be a warning to back off."

Victoria's eyes widened. "Do you think it's safe to continue the investigation?"

I looked around at the mess. "This just proves that I'm onto something. I can't let them scare me off. For Alice's sake, I have to keep going."

"I'll stand by you, Emma," Victoria said.

John returned with plywood and nails. He and Daniel set to board up the broken windows. The sound of the hammer echoed through the quiet bookstore. I called a glass contractor, arranging for new windows to be installed.

Chapter 20

The rhythmic thumping of hammers and buzzing of drills echoed through the air as contractors worked diligently to install the new glass windows for my bookstore. I stood outside the shop, watching over the work being done when a police car pulled up to the curb with a jolt. Detective Brown stepped out.

"Detective Brown," I greeted him. "What brings you here?"

He strode over to me, his face set in a grim line. "Emma, we need to talk."

I straightened up, bracing myself for whatever he had to say. "Sure, what's on your mind?"

He didn't waste any time. "You need to stop your snooping into Alice's death."

His bluntness took me aback. "Why? All I want is to help the police find out what happened to her. She was my best friend."

Detective Brown's eyes narrowed. "Your poking around is stirring up trouble. You're putting yourself in danger and complicating things for us. We have procedures to follow, and you're interfering."

"Complicating things? My bookstore has been vandalized and you think I'm the problem? Detective, I understand that you have your job to do, but I can't just sit by and do nothing. Alice deserves justice, and I won't stop until we find the killer."

He stepped closer, his expression hardening. "You don't understand the risks you're taking. These are dangerous people you're dealing with. You need to let us handle it."

I shook my head, my voice rising. "No, you don't understand! Alice was more than just a case to me. She was my friend, and I owe it to her to find out what happened. If that means I have to keep investigating, then so be it."

Detective Brown took another step closer. "Emma, you're not a detective. You're not trained for this. You're going to get yourself hurt, or worse. This isn't a game."

My hands clenched into fists at my sides, and I met his gaze. "I know it's not a game. This is my life, and it was Alice's life. I can't just turn my back on that."

His eyes flashed with frustration, and he exhaled sharply. "You're meddling in things you don't understand. You're making a mistake."

"Maybe," I shot back. "But it's a mistake I'm willing to make for Alice."

Detective Brown's jaw tightened. "You're stubborn. I'll give you that."

"This is about doing what's right, not about me, Detective."

The air was thick with tension as neither of us showed any sign of backing down. "Emma," he said, his voice low, "this is your last warning. Stop your investigation, or there will be consequences."

I glared at him. "I won't stop, Detective. Not until Alice's killer is brought to justice."

Detective Brown stared at me for a long moment, then turned on his heel and walked back to his car. I turned back to the contractors, who had paused their work to watch the confrontation. "Let's get those windows up so that we can open the bookstore," I said, my voice steady.

I observed as the contractors went back to their work, my heart racing in frustration. *Why did Detective Brown try to shut me down when I was making progress in unraveling the mystery?*

"Emma," Victoria's voice broke through my thoughts. "Are you okay?"

I let out a shaky breath. "No, Victoria, I'm not. Detective Brown tried to shut down my investigation, saying I'm a distraction to the police."

Victoria's eyes widened in disbelief. "That doesn't make any sense. Why would he do that?"

"I don't know. He said I was stirring up trouble and making people nervous. All I've done is follow the leads and try to help the police investigation. It's almost like he doesn't want me to find out the truth."

"Emma, you're making someone nervous, but it shouldn't be Detective Brown."

"Exactly. You would think he would welcome my assistance. Instead, he's trying to intimidate me."

"Take it easy, Emma. Maybe he's just having a rough day," Victoria said.

"I just don't understand why he's so adamant about stopping me. It's like he has a personal stake in this."

Chapter 21

The drive home was usually a peaceful break from a busy day at work. The steady purr of the engine and the familiar path brought me comfort. But today, my mind refused to slow down as I replayed Detective Brown's unexpected visit. Frustration boiled inside me, making it hard to concentrate on the road.

Suddenly, a screech of tires jolted me out of my thoughts. Before I could react, a pickup truck barreled into the right side of my car with a sickening crunch of metal. The world spun violently, and the last thing I saw was the shattered windshield before everything went black.

When I awoke, the antiseptic smell of a hospital room filled my nostrils. The beeping of monitors and the soft murmur of voices reached my ears. My head throbbed with a dull pain, and I felt disoriented.

"Emma? Babe, can you hear me?" Daniel's voice called gently. I turned my head and saw Daniel and Wyatt standing by my bedside, their faces etched with worry.

"Dan? Wyatt?" I croaked, my throat dry and scratchy. "What happened?"

Daniel leaned closer. "Your car was hit by a pickup truck. It was a hit-and-run. The police found you unconscious and brought you here."

"Where is Oliver?" I asked.

"Don't worry, Susan is watching over him," Wyatt reassured me.

I tried to sit up, but a wave of dizziness washed over me, and I sank back against the pillows. "A hit-and-run? Was it... deliberate?"

Wyatt stepped in. "We don't know yet. We are investigating, but it's suspicious, given everything that's been happening."

I closed my eyes, trying to recall the incident. "This can't be a coincidence. First the windows, now this. Someone's trying to stop me."

Daniel took my hand, his grip firm and comforting. "Babe, you need to rest. Let the police handle this."

"Did the person who killed Alice also try to kill me?" I whispered, opening my eyes to look at him.

Wyatt exchanged a glance with Daniel. "We'll look into it, Emma. But you need to rest."

I nodded, feeling the weight of exhaustion pressing down on me. "Okay. Promise me that you will find whoever did this. I know there are plenty of cameras along that road."

Daniel squeezed my hand. "You rest now, babe. We'll handle everything."

I lay back, feeling the pull of sleep tugging at me. I couldn't help but feel a flicker of fear. The danger was closer than ever, and now it was personal.

***

The morning light filtered through the hospital curtains. I blinked my eyes open, feeling the dull ache in my head and the stiffness in my muscles. The events of the previous day came rushing back, and I winced at the memory of the crash.

The door opened, and a doctor walked in, clipboard in hand and a smile on his face. "Good morning, Emma. How are you feeling?"

"Sore," I admitted, trying to sit up with a grimace. "But better, I think."

He glanced over his notes. "We observed you overnight, and it looks like you sustained only minor injuries. Some bruising and a mild concussion, but nothing too serious. You're free to go home today."

Relief washed over me. "Thank you, Doctor."

After the doctor left, I called my car insurance company to find out what my policy would cover.

"Ms. Wilson, do you have comprehensive and collision coverage?" the representative asked.

"Yes, I do."

"Good. Comprehensive and collision coverage will cover the repairs to your car, minus your deductible," she explained. "Since this was a hit-and-run, your uninsured motorist property damage coverage will also come into play. This will help cover the cost of the repairs if the driver at fault isn't found or doesn't have insurance."

"What about my hospital expenses? I have to stay at the hospital overnight because of my injuries."

"If you have personal injury protection or medical payments coverage, those will help cover your medical expenses, regardless of who was at fault," she said. "Uninsured motorist bodily injury coverage will also assist if the other driver is not identified or lacks insurance."

I thought back to when I had chosen my policy. "Yes, I have both personal injury protection and uninsured motorist coverage."

"Then you should be covered for both your car repairs and your medical expenses," she confirmed. "We'll need to process your claim and get all the necessary documentation, but it sounds like you have the coverage you need."

"Thank you. I'll gather all the documents and send them over as soon as I can."

Just as I ended the call, Daniel and Wyatt walked in. "How are you doing, babe?" Daniel asked, his eyes searching mine.

"I can go home today."

"Awesome!" Daniel beamed.

Wyatt gently squeezed my hand. "That's great, Emma. But take it easy, okay?"

I tried to sit up a little straighter. "Dan, my car is totaled. I'm going to need a new one."

Daniel nodded thoughtfully. "I was thinking, maybe we should lease a car for the short term. It'll give us some time to figure things out without rushing into a purchase."

I considered his suggestion. "That sounds like a good idea. Our car insurance should cover some of the cost. I talked to them earlier, and they said they'd handle the repairs. I didn't ask about the rental."

Before I could continue, two police officers entered the room. One was Officer Reynolds, whom I recognized from the vandalism investigation at the bookstore, and the other was a younger officer I didn't know.

"Good morning, Detective Miller. It's a pleasant surprise to see you here," Officer Reynolds greeted Wyatt.

"Good morning, officers. This is my sister, Emma," Wyatt introduced.

Officer Reynolds chuckled and said, "No wonder she has the same intensity as you, sir." He quickly apologized for his remark.

"No need to apologize," Wyatt smiled. "If anything, Emma is more intense than I am."

I couldn't help but roll my eyes at that comment, smiling nonetheless.

Officer Reynolds took a seat beside my bed. "Emma, your car accident happened at a four-way stop intersection. Witnesses said a pick-up truck ran the stop sign and hit your car. Unfortunately, the truck sped off before anyone could get a good look at the driver or the license plate number."

"I was driving home, navigating the familiar road. I remembered coming to a brief halt at the stop sign, but the pick-up truck came out of nowhere and collided with me on the right side in a T-bone fashion. Everything spun, and then it went black. I couldn't make out any details," I said.

"That's understandable," Officer Reynolds said. "Can you recall anything unusual about the truck? Any distinctive marks or colors?"

I closed my eyes, trying to pull the memory from the fog of my mind. "It was a dark color... maybe black or dark blue. And it was an older model, I think. But that's all I can remember."

Wyatt, who had been standing quietly by the window, stepped forward. "The truck must have sustained some damage in the collision. It'll need repairs. If we can check local auto repair shops, we might find a lead."

Officer Reynolds nodded. "We'll start checking repair shops in the area and see if anyone has brought in a truck matching Emma's description."

The younger officer looked up from his notepad. "Is there anyone you think might want to harm you? Any threats or conflicts recently?"

I sighed. "Yes, actually. My bookstore was vandalized three days ago. And I've been looking into the death of my friend, Alice Monroe. I think someone's trying to stop me."

The officers exchanged a look, their expressions growing more serious. "We'll look into this further," Officer Reynolds said. "In the meantime, be cautious. We'll increase patrols around your home and business."

"Thank you," I said.

As the officers left, Daniel turned to me. "You need to be more careful, Emma. This is getting dangerous."

"I know, but if I give up now, all of my hard work will have been for nothing. We're getting closer, and that's why they're trying to scare me."

"We'll find out who's behind this, Emma. But first, you need to take care of yourself," Wyatt said.

I managed a weak smile. "It seems like everything has been going wrong lately. First, Alice died suddenly, then my bookstore was vandalized, and to top it off, I was in a car accident. Am I just losing my mind?" Tears rolled down my cheeks as I struggled to make sense of everything.

Daniel wrapped his arms around me. "You're not losing your mind, babe. But maybe you've taken on too much."

"I agree," added Wyatt. "We've been talking, and we think it's time for you to stop the investigation."

Feeling betrayed, I glared at them. "So you've been talking behind my back?"

They both shrugged, unable to deny it.

"So you've joined force with Detective Brown and are now on his side?" I pressed on.

Daniel raised his hands in surrender. "We are on your side, of course, but we also want to make sure you don't get hurt again, babe."

Just then, the door opened again, and Eleanor and Avery walked in, each holding a bouquet of flowers. Their faces brightened when they saw me, and they hurried over to my bedside.

"Oh, Emma!" Eleanor exclaimed, placing the flowers on the table next to me. "We were so worried when we heard."

"How are you feeling?" Avery asked, arranging the flowers in a vase and setting them by the window where the sunlight streamed in.

"Better now that you're all here," I said, smiling at my friends. "Thank you for the flowers. They're beautiful."

"Do you need anything? Can we help with anything at the bookstore?" Eleanor asked.

"No, thank you. The doctor said that I could go home today."

"That's great! We'll take care of everything, don't you worry. You just focus on getting better," Avery said.

Chapter 22

On a brisk Saturday morning, Daniel, Oliver, and I loaded up the car and headed to Atlanta to visit Daniel's parents. Their home was a sprawling two-story colonial, with white pillars lining the wide porch that wrapped around the front. Ivy clung to the brick exterior, giving it a timeless charm.

We got out of the car, and Oliver immediately ran toward the front door. "Grandma! Grandpa!" he called out.

The front door opened, and Daniel's mother, Margaret, stepped out to greet us.

"There's my favorite grandson!" Margaret bent down to scoop Oliver into her arms, wincing slightly from the recent surgery but refusing to let it dampen her spirits.

"Hi, Grandma!" Oliver exclaimed, wrapping his little arms around her neck. "Did you miss me?"

"Oh, I missed you so much, sweetheart. You've grown even more handsome since I last saw you."

"Hi, Mom," Daniel said, embracing her gently. "How are you feeling?"

"I'm doing alright. Just taking it one day at a time. It's wonderful to see you all."

I hugged Margaret before we walked inside. The foyer was spacious, with high ceilings and a grand staircase leading up to the second floor.

Daniel's father, Robert, appeared from the kitchen. "Welcome, welcome!" he said, giving us each a hug. "We've missed you. Can I get anyone something to drink?"

"It's good to be here. How are you holding up?" I asked.

"As well as can be expected," Robert replied. "We're just grateful the surgery went well."

We settled into the cozy living room. Oliver played with the toys on the rug and Margaret sat beside me on the couch.

"How are you feeling, Margaret?" I asked.

She looked tired, the pallor of her skin a reminder of her surgery. "I'm doing okay, Emma. The surgery went well. They removed the melanoma, and the doctor is optimistic. I'm starting chemotherapy next week."

I reached out, placing a comforting hand on hers. "I'm so glad the surgery went well. How are you feeling about the chemo?"

She squeezed my hand. "It's daunting, to be honest. But I'm ready to fight."

"Just give me a call if you need anything. I'll come over and lend a hand with whatever needs to be done," I offered. "I can help with cooking, cleaning, or anything else that might make things easier for you. It's only an hour's drive to come here."

Margaret smiled gratefully. "Thank you, Emma. I know how hectic it can be running a bookstore. Just having you all here today has lifted my spirits."

***

The sun hung low in the sky as I stood in the spacious kitchen, preparing dinner. I had decided to make one of my favorite meals: chicken pot pie with a side of roasted vegetables.

As I chopped the vegetables, the sound of laughter floated in from the backyard. I glanced out the window and saw Daniel working in the yard, his sleeves rolled up. He was clearing away fallen leaves and tidying up the flower beds. From a distance, I could hear Oliver's high-pitched giggles as he tossed a ball back and forth with his grandfather. I smiled to myself, feeling a sense of peace I hadn't felt in weeks.

The aroma of the chicken filling mingled with the scent of fresh herbs as I sautéed them in a large skillet. I added a splash of white wine, letting it simmer, the rich scent enveloping the kitchen. As I readied the pie crust, I rolled out the dough, carefully placing it over the chicken filling before crimping the edges. Cooking had been my way of showing love and care, and today was no different.

Just when I was about to slide the pie into the oven, Daniel walked in, wiping his hands on a rag. He leaned against the counter. "Smells amazing in here."

"How's the yard looking?" I asked, returning his smile.

"Much better. I took care of a poison ivy that was creeping around."

I put the pie inside the oven and set a timer. "You got to be careful with that plant. Did you wear gloves while handling it?"

"Yep, I did. It's all disposed of and taken care of."

"It seems like Oliver is having a blast with your dad."

Daniel chuckled. "Yeah, they're thick as thieves. It's good for him to spend time with his grandparents."

I walked over and wrapped my arms around him, resting my head on his chest. "This place feels like a sanctuary," I whispered. "I needed this."

He held me close. "We all did."

The timer beeped, pulling me back to the present. I reluctantly let go of Daniel and pulled the pie out of the oven, the golden crust bubbling and crisp. I placed the steaming pie on the table, alongside a platter of roasted vegetables.

"Dinner's ready!" I called out.

"Mom and Dad are going to love this chicken pot pie," Daniel said.

"I hope so. It's been a while since I made this, but it seemed like the perfect dish for tonight."

We carried the dishes to the dining room, where Robert, Margaret, and Oliver were already seated. Margaret smiled brightly when she saw the pie. "I've been looking forward to this all day."

"I wanted to make something hearty for tonight," I said, placing the pie in the center of the table.

Robert leaned in, inhaling deeply. "If it tastes half as good as it smells, we're in for a treat."

"Can I have a big piece, Mommy?" Oliver asked.

"Of course, little man." I cut a big portion for him and placed it on his plate. "Be careful. It's hot."

We took our seats around the table, and Daniel served generous portions of the chicken pot pie onto each plate. The first bite was met with a chorus of appreciative murmurs.

"This is delicious, Emma," Margaret said.

I blushed. "I'm glad you like it. It's one of my favorite recipes."

Robert nodded enthusiastically, taking another bite. "The crust is just the right amount of flaky, and the filling is so flavorful. You'll have to share the recipe with us."

Daniel chuckled. "I've been trying to get her to write it down for years. Maybe you'll have better luck, Dad."

"This reminds me of the pot pie my mother used to make," Robert said, leaning back in his chair. "She always used fresh herbs from her garden. It adds such a wonderful depth of flavor."

Margaret nodded. "I remember that. She had the greenest thumb of anyone I've ever known. Everything she grew was robust."

"I've been trying to grow my herbs," I admitted. "But I'm not sure I have the magic touch. They're still alive, though, so that's a start."

Robert raised his glass. "To Emma, the best cook of this family."

Chapter 23

The Atlanta Aquarium was alive with energy and activity. A sea of excited families and children milled about. The towering glass walls and vibrant marine exhibits promised a day of wonder, a perfect way to end our visit before heading back to Athens. Daniel, Oliver, and I made our way through the crowds, following the signs that led to the dolphin show.

The amphitheater was immense, with rows of seats circling a massive pool that shimmered under the bright lights. We found our seats near the front, and I could feel Oliver's excitement radiating beside me. His eyes were wide with anticipation as he clutched his small dolphin plushie, a souvenir from the gift shop.

The lights dimmed, and a hush fell over the audience. The music began, a lively tune that matched the bubbling excitement in the air. Suddenly, with a splash and a burst of energy, the dolphins appeared. They leaped gracefully from the water, their sleek bodies cutting through the air in perfect arcs. The audience erupted in applause, and Oliver's face lit up with pure delight.

The trainers guided the dolphins through a series of incredible tricks. They soared high into the air, spinning and twisting before diving back into the pool with hardly a splash.

"Did you see that, Mommy? dolphins jumped out of water!" Oliver exclaimed, bouncing in his seat.

"They did, little man. I'm so glad we got to see this."

Daniel leaned over. "It's nice to see him so happy."

At one point, a trainer stood on the back of two dolphins as they glided across the water, drawing gasps and cheers from the crowd. The dolphins responded to the trainers' commands with enthusiasm, their intelligence and agility on full display.

As the music swelled to a climax, the dolphins finished the performance with a dramatic leap, soaring high above the water before diving back down with a tremendous splash. The audience erupted into applause, and I found myself clapping, caught up in the sheer joy of the moment.

After the dolphin show, we visited the local wildlife preservation section at the aquarium. Tucked away in a corner, the exhibit was a refreshing retreat of verdant greenery, babbling fountains, and lively artwork. We stopped at a display featuring local fish species and their habitats. An aquarium employee, a young woman with a bright smile and a name tag that read "Megan," noticed Oliver's wide-eyed curiosity and approached us.

"Hello there!" she greeted, kneeling to Oliver's level. "I'm Megan. What's your name?"

"My name is Oliver."

"Do you like learning about animals?"

Oliver nodded, clutching his dolphin plushie. "Yes! I liked the dolphins. What's this?" He pointed to a tank filled with colorful fish darting among the aquatic plants.

Megan smiled. "These are some of the fish that live in our local rivers and lakes. Did you know that it's really important to keep their homes clean and safe?"

Oliver looked up at her. "Why?"

"Well, just like how you need a nice, clean place to live, so do these fish. If we let trash and harmful chemicals get into the water, it can make the fish sick and even destroy their homes. That's why we have to be careful about what we put into our rivers and lakes."

I watched as Oliver absorbed her words. "How can we help?" I asked.

Megan's smile widened. "That's a great question! We can help by not littering and by recycling things like plastic and paper. We can also use less water and tell other people how important it is to keep our rivers and lakes clean. Every little bit helps."

"I want to help the fishies," Olive declared.

Megan laughed softly. "That's wonderful, Oliver. You can be a big help, even just by doing small things. And when you grow up, you can teach others too."

As Megan continued to explain the fragile state of our local wildlife and the urgent need for immediate action to preserve our environment, I felt a deep sense of connection to Alice's cause. Her unwavering dedication and tireless efforts to protect the environment became even more admirable now that I had a better understanding of its significance from Megan's words. A fierce determination surged through me, urging me to carry on her legacy.

Chapter 24

The drive to Alice's apartment was steeped in a heavy silence, broken only by occasional sniffles from Mary who clutched the spare key in her hand.

When we arrived, I parked the car and we sat for a moment. "Are you alright?" I asked softly.

"Yes, I think so. Thank you for coming with me, Emma. I couldn't do this alone."

"Of course, Mary."

We made our way up the stairs to Alice's apartment. Mary hesitated for a moment at the door before unlocking it and pushing it open. The familiar scent of Alice's favorite lavender air freshener hit us. Stepping inside, I was struck by how much the apartment still felt like Alice. The walls were adorned with photos from her travels, and her coffee mug sat on the kitchen counter as if waiting for her return.

Mary stood in the middle of the living room. "It's like she's still here."

My throat tightened as I nodded in agreement. "I miss her so much."

We started in the living room, sorting through Alice's belongings. Each item we touched seemed to tell a story, reminding me of the vibrant woman she had been. I picked up a framed photo of us from college, our arms around each other and big smiles on our faces. Tears blurred my vision as I remembered the day it was taken.

Mary and I worked in silence, the only sound the soft thud of objects as we packed them into boxes.

As we worked through the rooms, the home office stood as a clear testament to Alice's dedication to her work. Various awards and certificates decorated the walls, showcasing her accomplishments. I sifted through her desk and when I opened one of the lower drawers, my heart skipped a beat. There, resting on top of a stack of documents, was a large envelope with my name scrawled across it in Alice's familiar handwriting.

"Mary, look at this," I said, holding up the envelope. "It's addressed to me."

Mary leaned in to get a closer look. "Emma, she must have wanted you to have it. It could be important."

The weight of the envelope in my hands felt significant. "I think I should take it home before opening it," I said softly.

"Of course, Emma. Whatever you think is best."

As we locked up and left the apartment, I held the envelope against my chest. The drive home was quiet, each of us lost in our thoughts.

Once I returned home, I sank into my favorite armchair and placed the envelope on my lap. Daniel and Oliver were out running errands. I took a deep breath before carefully tearing open the envelope. Inside, I found a stack of documents, photographs, and a handwritten letter from Alice. My hands trembled as I unfolded the letter, recognizing her neat script immediately.

Dear Emma,

If you're reading this, it means I'm no longer here, and my fears have come true. I'm so sorry to put this burden on you, but you're the only person I trust with my life's work. What I've uncovered is massive—Gregory Hale's construction company is involved in the illegal dumping of toxic waste into the river. I've collected enough evidence to expose them, but I'm being watched, and I fear for my life.

Emma, thank you for being the best friend I could ever ask for. You were there for me through thick and thin, and your support and love meant the world to me. I wish I could tell you this in person, to see your reassuring smile one more time.

In this envelope, you'll find all the evidence I've gathered— reports, photographs, recordings. Please take this to the authorities. Make sure they can't ignore it. I know it's dangerous, but I also know you have the strength and courage to see this through.

I miss you already, Emma. I miss our late-night talks, our shared dreams, our laughter. I wish with all my heart that we could have more time together. Maybe in the next life, we'll find each other again and be friends once more.

Please, be careful. These people are powerful and ruthless. But I believe in you. I believe in us. You're my hero, Emma.

With all my love,
Alice

Tears blurred my vision as I finished reading the letter. Alice had trusted me with her life's work, her final plea for justice. I carefully laid out the documents and photographs, my mind racing as I absorbed the information. There were detailed reports, photographs of the dumping sites, and even recordings of conversations implicating key figures in the scandal.

Chapter 25

I sat down at the kitchen table, holding Alice's letter tightly in my hand. Daniel sat across from me, deep in thought as he pored over the documents that Alice had entrusted to me.

"Babe," he said, breaking the silence, "this evidence is damning. It clearly shows Gregory Hale's construction company is involved in illegal dumping. However, it doesn't directly prove his involvement in Alice's death."

"I know, Dan. But it shows a motive and connects the dots. We need to take this to Wyatt. He'll know what to do with it."

Daniel leaned back in his chair, running a hand through his hair. "You're right. Wyatt will know where to take this evidence."

Later that evening, we called Wyatt and asked to meet him at our house.

The doorbell rang, and Daniel got up to let Wyatt in. Moments later, my brother stepped into the living room.

"Hey, Wyatt," I greeted him.

"What's going on?" Wyatt replied, taking a seat across from us.

I handed him the envelope and the letter. "This is from Alice. I found it in her apartment. It's evidence of Gregory Hale's company's dumping of toxic wastes into the river."

Wyatt's eyes widened as he unfolded the letter and documents and began to read. The room was silent except for the sound of the paper rustling. As Wyatt read, his expression grew more serious, and by the time he finished, his jaw was set in a grim line.

"This is incriminating," he said, looking up at us. "It's clear evidence that Gregory's company was involved in illegal dumping. Alice must have been planning to expose him."

I felt a surge of emotion. "Alice was trying to do the right thing, and it cost her life."

Daniel leaned forward. "Gregory had everything to lose if this came out. His business, his reputation—everything. Killing Alice was a way to silence her and protect himself."

Wyatt nodded. "Gregory's motive is clear. By eliminating Alice, he stopped her from publishing her findings, which would have led to severe penalties for his company and a huge scandal. It makes perfect sense from his twisted perspective. What we have is more than enough to launch an investigation into Gregory's activities. But it doesn't directly tie him to Alice's death."

"How do we go from here?" I asked. "We have this letter and the evidence of the dumping, but can we determine if Gregory is directly involved in Alice's murder?"

Wyatt considered the question. "We have to find someone who can testify that Gregory knew about Alice's investigation and felt threatened by it. If we can establish that he had both the motive and the opportunity, it strengthens our case."

"With the resources at his disposal, obtaining animal tranquilizers and a dart gun would be easy for Gregory. If we can find a witness or some correspondence that ties him to the murder weapon, it should be enough to bring him to justice," Daniel said.

"Maybe someone in his company knew about it. An employee or a confidant who might have overheard something. We need to dig deeper," I said.

Wyatt gave me a reassuring smile. "I'll hand these pieces of evidence over to Detective Brown and we'll launch a full investigation into Gregory Hale's company. We may have to involve environmental agencies. You need to be careful, both of you. If Gregory is involved, he won't hesitate to protect himself."

"We will," Daniel assured him.

After Wyatt left, I felt a sense of hope mingled with a lingering fear. Daniel pulled me into an embrace, his warmth and strength grounding me.

"We're getting close," I said, my head resting against his chest.

"The shit is about to hit the fan."

Chapter 26

It's early morning, and the town was just beginning to stir. I unlocked the front door of the bookstore and was about to step inside when I noticed a man walking toward me.

My heart skipped a beat as I recognized him from his TV appearances. Gregory Hale. He was taller than I had expected, with a lean, almost gaunt frame. His graying hair was neatly combed, and he wore a gray suit that did little to soften the sharp angles of his face. His brown eyes were cold.

"Good morning, Emma," he said. "May I have a word with you in private?"

My heart raced. The man standing before me was the prime suspect in Alice's death, yet here he was, asking to speak with me alone. The rational part of my brain screamed caution, warning me of the potential danger of letting him into the bookstore. The thought of being alone with him sent a shiver down my spine. Yet, there was another part of me that saw this as a rare opportunity. The bookstore was located on a busy street; if something went wrong, I could call for help. This was my chance to confront him directly, to look into his eyes and ask him point-blank if he had anything to do with Alice's death. After a few agonizing moments of internal debate, I made my decision.

"Alright, Gregory," I said, trying to keep my voice steady. "Come in."

I opened the door wider, allowing him to step inside. He glanced around the bookstore, his eyes sweeping the shelves and displays as if assessing every detail. I led him to the large sofa at the center of the store.

Before sitting down, Gregory looked around again, making sure there were no security cameras inside. His scrutiny made me uneasy, but I remained composed. We sat down, the plush cushions sinking under our weight.

"What can I do for you?" I asked.

He leaned back, crossing one leg over the other. "I'm aware that you've been digging into my business affairs, Emma. You and your little group of friends seem quite determined to uncover something you shouldn't."

I swallowed hard, my heart pounding. "We're just seeking the truth, Gregory. Alice Monroe was a dear friend of mine."

Gregory's eyes narrowed, and he leaned forward, his expression turning icy. "Your friend Alice was playing with fire. She should have known better than to meddle in matters that didn't concern her."

I felt a surge of anger but kept my voice calm. "She was trying to protect our community and environment." I took a deep breath, gathering my courage. "Gregory, did you murder Alice Monroe?"

Gregory's eyes flashed with a mixture of anger and surprise. For a moment, he seemed taken aback by my directness. Then he composed himself, a slick smile spreading across his face. "Emma, I would never do such a thing. Alice's death was a tragedy, but I had nothing to do with it."

I stared at him, trying to read the truth behind his cold eyes. "She was about to expose your company's dumping of toxic wastes into the river. That's a strong motive for murder."

Gregory's smile widened. "You're mistaken. My company operates within the bounds of the law. And as for Alice, her death has nothing to do with me. But I see you're very passionate about your little investigation."

He leaned forward, his gaze intense. "How about I make you an offer? I'll donate $50,000 to your bookstore. Think of what you could do with that money. New books, better facilities, more community events. All you have to do is stop snooping around."

The offer hung in the air, a tempting but poisoned chalice. I felt a surge of anger at his audacity. "My bookstore doesn't need your money. What it needs is justice for Alice."

Gregory's smile vanished, replaced by a look of cold fury. "You're making a big mistake, Emma. You have no idea who you're dealing with."

I refused to be intimidated. "I know exactly who I'm dealing with. You're a man who thinks he can buy his way out of anything, who thinks he's above the law. But you're wrong. I won't stop until Alice's killer is brought to justice."

His eyes narrowed, his voice low and threatening. "You're playing a dangerous game, Emma. People who cross me tend to regret it."

"Maybe you're the one who should be worried, Gregory. The truth has a way of coming out, no matter how hard you try to bury it. I'm not going to let Alice's death be in vain."

He stood up abruptly, his eyes flashing with anger. "You'll regret this, Emma. Mark my words."

As he turned and walked out of the bookstore, I felt a mixture of relief and dread. Gregory Hale was desperate, and his threats only confirmed that we were on the right path.

Chapter 27

The phone interrupted my thoughts with its shrill ring. I hesitated before answering. "Emma's Haven, how can I help you?"

"Ms. Wilson, we need to talk," an urgent voice said. It sounded familiar, but I couldn't place it.

"Who is this?"

"It's Sam. We talked a few days ago about Alice. Can you meet me at the park on Maple Street in an hour? I'll explain everything then."

"Wait, why can't we meet at my bookstore?" I asked, but the line had already gone dead.

I sat there for a moment. There was a flicker of fear, but I remembered Sam's last call that had brought so much to light.

Nestled in the heart of downtown, the small park on Maple Street provided a peaceful escape. When I arrived at noon, the sun shone bright, filtering through the leaves of towering oak trees and casting shadows across the grass. In the center of the park was a tranquil pond, with ducks gliding smoothly across its surface and lily pads dotting the water. I scanned the area for any sign of the caller, but no one stood out. I walked toward a bench near the pond, my nerves on edge.

"Ms. Wilson?" a voice called softly.

I turned to see a man approaching. He was average height and well-dressed, with an air of tension about him.

"My name is Samuel Lewis. Alice and I were friends before she passed away."

I raised my eyebrows in surprise. "Hold on, you're Samuel Lewis? You're the one who called me?"

"Yes," he confirmed with a nod.

"A few days back, my friend and I visited your house and spoke with your wife, Chloe. She was still upset about your affair with Alice," I looked directly into his eyes.

Samuels' face turned red. He looked around to ensure we weren't overheard. "Alice and I were both deeply involved in environmental activism. We met at several events and worked together on various projects. We had a one-night stand, but it was a mistake. We remained friends after that, strictly professional. I apologize for the way my wife acted during your visit, but she did not murder Alice."

"What do you want to tell me today? Why didn't you disclose the information to the authorities?"

"Because I was afraid," Samuel admitted. "Not of the affair coming to light, but of what Alice was uncovering. She told me about Gregory Hale's illegal dumping. She was gathering evidence, and I thought she was getting too close. I didn't want to become a target too."

"So you knew she was in danger, and you didn't do anything to help her?"

Samuel's face fell, guilt written in every line. "I didn't realize how serious it was until it was too late. I thought she was being paranoid, but now... I think she was right."

"Why are you telling me this now?" I asked. "Why come forward now?"

"Because I can't live with the guilt," he said, his eyes pleading with me. "Alice was a good person, and she didn't deserve what happened to her. I want to help. I have information that might be useful. I just... I don't know who else to trust."

I took a deep breath. "What kind of information?"

Samuel hesitated, glancing around as if the trees themselves might be listening. "Alice mentioned a place where Gregory Hale's company was dumping the waste," he said slowly. "There's a landmark by the river—an old, abandoned boathouse. She said that was the most recent dumping site."

"An abandoned boathouse? I don't recall seeing anything about that in the envelope Alice left me. The evidence I saw points to various sites, but nothing about a boathouse."

"Gregory's company is crafty. They use evasive strategies, constantly changing their dumping sites to avoid detection. The abandoned boathouse is their latest spot. Alice was actively investigating it before she died," Samuel said.

"Did Alice say anything else about the boathouse?" I asked.

"She didn't have a chance to compile everything. She was gathering more evidence when she... when she was killed."

I stared at the ground, my mind racing. "The abandoned boathouse could be the final piece of evidence we need to expose Gregory and his company."

"Yes. If Gregory finds out we're onto him, there's no telling what he might do to protect his interests."

"Samuel, this is vital information. You need to tell my brother Wyatt. He's a detective with the Athens Police Department," I said.

He shook his head. "I don't know. If I get involved, it could be dangerous for me and my family."

I reached out, placing a hand on his arm. "I understand your fear, Samuel. But if we don't act now, more people could get hurt. Alice trusted you with this information. She believed in you. And now I need you to do the right thing."

He looked down. "Alice was brave, braver than I ever was."

"Then honor her bravery now," I urged. "Help us bring her killer to justice. Help us stop them from harming anyone else."

Samuel sighed. "Okay. What should I do?"

"Go to the police station and inform them that you have important information for Detective Wyatt Miller."

"Can you come with me?" Samuel asked.

"Not today. I have urgent matters to attend to."

Chapter 28

When Daniel and I arrived at the abandoned boathouse, a sense of foreboding settled over me. The old structure sat on the edge of the river, its once-proud wooden beams weathered and gray with age. The roof sagged in the middle, patches of sunlight filtering through the gaps. Ivy and weeds had claimed the structure, winding their way up the walls and through the cracks in the floorboards. Late afternoon sunlight illuminated every detail of the run-down building.

Anxiety and nervousness flooded my heart as I looked over at Daniel. "This is it. This could be the final piece of the puzzle."

Daniel reached over and took my hand. "We don't have to do this alone, babe. We can wait for the police. Let them handle it."

I shook my head. "We've come this far, Dan. We need to see this through, for Alice."

He sighed. "I know, but I don't want you to get hurt. This could be dangerous."

I leaned closer to him and pressed my lips against his, feeling a wave of gratitude for his unwavering support. "I love you, Dan. But I have to do this."

He kissed me back, his hand cupping my cheek. "I know. I love you too."

With a final squeeze of his hand, I stepped out of the car. Daniel followed, his eyes scanning the area for any signs of danger. The ground was uneven, covered in patches of grass and loose gravel.

"This place gives me the creeps," Daniel muttered. "But if we're going to find anything, it'll be here."

"We'll be in and out. Just long enough to find the evidence we need," I said.

We walked inside, the wooden floor groaning under our weight. The interior was dim, despite the sunlight streaming through the gaps in the walls and roof. Old, rusted tools and broken furniture were scattered about. The river lapped gently against the side of the boathouse, its sound almost soothing in the otherwise silent space. The air was thick with the smell of damp earth and something more acrid, a chemical scent that made my stomach turn. Daniel and I exchanged a worried glance.

I navigated the clutter. "Look for anything that seems recent. Containers, chemicals, wastes, anything that could tie to Gregory Hale's company."

We split up, each of us taking a side of the boathouse. I moved toward a corner where several old barrels were stacked haphazardly. As I got closer, the chemical smell grew stronger, confirming my suspicion. I noticed a few newer-looking containers mixed in with the older ones, their surfaces clean and free of the grime that coated everything else.

"Daniel, over here," I called, pointing to the containers. "These look recent."

He hurried over, and together we examined the barrels. They were marked with hazardous material symbols and labels identifying Gregory Hale's construction company. The toxic waste was seeping through the wooden floor and into the river below. A shiver ran down my spine as I realized what this meant. "This is it," I whispered. "This is the proof we need."

My heart raced as I snapped photos with my phone, documenting the evidence. "We've got them."

Just as I finished taking the photos, the sound of footsteps on the gravel outside made us freeze. The hairs on the back of my neck stood on end as I turned slowly. Before we could react, the door to the boathouse swung open with a loud creak.

Gregory Hale and Lucas Scott stood in the doorway. Their faces contorted with anger and Gregory held a gun in his hand. His sharp brown eyes glinted coldly.

"Well, well, what do we have here?" Gregory sneered. "Looks like the little detective and her husband have been snooping around where they shouldn't be."

My heart pounded in my chest and I tried to keep my voice steady. "We know what you're doing, Gregory. We have proof of your illegal dumping. It's over."

Gregory's eyes narrowed, and he took a step closer, the gun never wavering. "You think a few pictures and barrels are going to bring me down? You're more naive than I thought. You've underestimated what I'm capable of. I've built my company from the ground up, and I wasn't going to let some environmental crusaders take it all away."

Lucas stepped forward. "You should have stayed out of it, Emma. Now you've put yourself and your husband in a very dangerous position."

Daniel shielded me with his body. "What do you want, Gregory?"

Gregory's smile didn't reach his eyes. "I could ask you the same thing. Trespassing on private property, poking your noses where they don't belong. It's not very wise."

"Let Emma go, Gregory," Daniel said, his voice firm.

Gregory laughed. "You've become quite the thorn in my side, Emma. It's time to remove it."

I glanced around, desperately searching for an escape or a way to disarm him. "Alice was onto you. She knew you were dumping toxic waste into the river, and now everyone else knows too. The police are already on their way."

Gregory's face twisted with rage, and he raised the gun higher. "You're lying. But it doesn't matter. By the time they find you, I'll be long gone."

Daniel's jaw tightened. "You've destroyed lives to get what you want. Alice discovered your illegal activities, and you killed her for it."

For a moment, a flicker of something—perhaps guilt or regret—crossed Gregory's face, but it vanished as quickly as it appeared. "Alice was a problem that needed to be solved. She couldn't keep her nose out of other people's business. Just like you two."

"You can't hide forever, Gregory. The truth will come out," I said.

"You're brave, I'll give you that. But bravery won't save you now."

"Gregory, you don't have to do this," I said.

"Emma, dear, you still don't get it, do you?" Gregory's lip curled into a smile. "There's nothing you can do. You're completely at my mercy."

I hated the way he said my name as if we were old friends instead of adversaries on opposite sides of a moral chasm. "Mercy? Please, Gregory, there's been enough violence. Think of your reputation—"

"Reputation?" he cut me off with a bark of laughter. "Once I'm done with you two, there won't be anyone left to question my reputation."

Daniel's voice cut through the tense air. "Gregory, think about what you're doing. You have money and influence— you don't want to add murder to your name."

"My name?" Gregory scoffed. "The only thing I'm concerned with is keeping my affairs private, and you two are threatening that privacy."

Daniel pressed on. "Are you out of your mind, Gregory? Do you think you can get away with murder? You're delusional. There are consequences. You can't just—"

"Consequences?" Gregory interrupted. "I make the consequences. Alice was a fool to think she could stop me. And now, you're about to join her."

My heart hammered against my ribs. I forced myself to meet Gregory's gaze. "The police know everything, Gregory. It's only a matter of time before they arrest you."

"You think I'm afraid of the police? I've been one step ahead of them for years. Alice was nothing more than a minor inconvenience. We ambushed her, shot her with an animal tranquilizer gun, and made it look like an accidental drowning. Evidence can be... misplaced or destroyed. People can be silenced."

The confession hit me like a physical blow, the horror of Alice's final moments crashing over me. I felt the raw edges of grief tear at my heart. "You're a monster," I spat. "Alice was a good person."

Gregory's expression darkened, and he stepped closer. "Good people don't matter in this world. Power does. Control does."

"If you shoot us, the police will trace the bullets back to your gun through forensic ballistics. Put down the gun, Gregory," I said.

Lucas stopped pacing and looked at Gregory, uncertainty flickering in his eyes. "Greg, maybe she's right. This is getting out of hand. We need to think about our next move."

Gregory's grip tightened on the gun, his knuckles white. "Our next move is to make sure these two can't talk. We finish this, once and for all."

Just then, the distant sound of sirens reached us, growing louder with each passing second. Gregory's eyes widened, panic seeping into his confident facade. "No, no, no," he muttered, glancing around frantically. "We need more time."

Daniel's voice rose above the chaos. "It's over, Gregory. You hear that? The police are coming."

"Gregory, drop the gun. Don't make it worse than it already is," I said.

For a moment, I saw the flicker of indecision in Gregory's eyes.

The doors of the boathouse burst open, and police officers swarmed in, weapons drawn. Wyatt was at the forefront. "Freeze! Drop your weapon!"

With a look of utter defeat, Gregory lowered the gun, his shoulders slumping. His face was a mask of despair as the officers moved in to arrest him and Lucas.

Wyatt hurried over to us. "Are you two okay?"

I nodded, tears of relief streaming down my face. "We're okay. We got them, Wyatt. We got them."

"Once again, you scared the crap out of me, sis," Wyatt said.

"How did you know I was here?" I winked.

"Samuel Lewis came to the station and told me about this place. When you didn't answer your phone, we traced your location. When I saw where you were, I knew things could get out of hand quickly. So, I called for all available units to come to this boathouse," Wyatt explained.

"I didn't realize you called. I must have been too focused on our conversation with Gregory," I admitted.

"I don't think Gregory would have let you answer Wyatt's call," Daniel teased.

As the officers led Gregory and Lucas away, I collapsed into Daniel's arms, the weight of the ordeal finally crashing down on me. We had done it. We had brought Alice's killers to justice.

Chapter 29

As we prepared for our picnic in Riverside Park, the sun bathed everything in a golden hue. We chose a spot near the river, where the water flowed gently, reflecting the shimmering sunlight like a thousand tiny diamonds. Families paddled canoes along the water, and children splashed at the edge, their joyful squeals echoing through the park. The riverbank was lined with tall willows, their branches swaying in the breeze.

Daniel spread out a picnic blanket on the soft grass, while Oliver ran around excitedly. Wyatt, Benjamin, Eleanor, and Avery joined us, carrying baskets filled with fresh sandwiches, fruit salads, and baked sweets.

"Look at this place," Eleanor said, spreading out a blanket. "It's beautiful."

I smiled. "It really is. There's something magical about Riverside Park."

Daniel handed me a sandwich, and I took a bite, savoring the fresh flavors.

Oliver ran over with a handful of wildflowers, presenting them to me with a proud grin. "Mommy, look what I found!"

"They're beautiful, Ollie," I said, pulling him into a hug.

Eleanor retrieved her phone from her pocket and brought it closer to me.

"What is it?" I asked, sitting up.

"You have to see this," Eleanor said, passing her phone to me. "It's an article from the Athens Chronicle, written by Penelope Green."

I took the phone from her, curiosity piqued. My heart raced as I began to read the article, Eleanor and the others leaning in close.

Gregory Hale's Construction Company Caught Illegally Dumping Toxic Waste into River
By Penelope Green

Athens, Georgia — In a shocking revelation that has sent ripples through our community, Gregory Hale's construction company has been exposed for illegally dumping toxic waste into the river for years. This clandestine operation has not only violated numerous environmental regulations but has also posed significant risks to public health and the local ecosystem.

An investigation led by this newspaper, supported by independent environmental activists, has uncovered irrefutable evidence of this egregious malpractice.

Documents obtained from inside sources, as well as physical evidence collected from multiple sites along the river, paint a damning picture of corporate greed and environmental negligence.

The Illegal Dumping Operation

For a few years, Hale's construction company has been covertly disposing of hazardous waste generated from its various projects into the river. According to sources within the company, the decision to illegally dump these materials was driven by a desire to cut costs. Proper disposal of hazardous waste is expensive, requiring adherence to stringent safety protocols and regulations. By bypassing these procedures, Hale's company saved millions of dollars, enhancing their profit margins at the expense of the environment and public health.

The Path to Justice

This newspaper's investigation, bolstered by the evidence and the whistleblower's testimony, has prompted local authorities to take immediate action. Environmental agencies are conducting a thorough review of Hale's operations, and legal proceedings are expected to follow.

Gregory Hale, a prominent figure in the business community, has long enjoyed a reputation as a successful and influential entrepreneur. These revelations, however, cast a dark shadow over his legacy. Hale has denied any wrongdoing, claiming that he was unaware of the illegal dumping. However, the evidence suggests otherwise.

Investigating a Tragic Death

In a related development, the police are also investigating whether Gregory Hale is involved in the murder and drowning of our colleague and beloved journalist Alice Monroe. Alice was a dedicated reporter who was working on a story about illegal dumping in the river before her untimely death. Her body was found in the very river now known to be contaminated by Hale's company's waste.

The circumstances surrounding Alice's death have raised many questions, and the community is demanding answers. Police sources indicate that new evidence has come to light, potentially linking Hale to this tragic event. If proven, this connection could result in even more severe charges against him.

Community Response

The community's response has been swift and vocal. Environmental groups are calling for stringent penalties and comprehensive cleanup efforts. Residents, shocked and outraged, are demanding accountability and transparency.

"We trusted these companies to act responsibly," said Emma Wilson, a local bookstore owner and environmental activist who has been instrumental in bringing this issue to light. "This betrayal of trust is devastating, but we will fight to ensure justice is served."

Conclusion

As this story continues to unfold, one thing is clear: the fight for environmental justice is far from over. The exposure of Gregory Hale's illegal dumping practices is a significant victory, but it is only the beginning. Our community must remain vigilant, holding those in power accountable and working together to protect our precious natural resources. The investigation into Alice Monroe's death adds a somber urgency to the matter, reminding us all of the personal costs involved in the pursuit of truth and justice.

Penelope Green,
Staff Writer,
Athens Chronicle

"Unbelievable," I muttered, shaking my head.

Wyatt, who had been talking to Benjamin, looked over with interest. "What's going on?"

I handed him the phone. "Penelope wrote an article exposing Gregory Hale's illegal dumping."

Avery spoke up. "I always knew Gregory was greedy, but this… this is beyond anything I imagined. He put so many lives at risk just to save a few bucks."

Eleanor nodded. "He thought he could get away with this."

"People like Gregory Hale think they're untouchable. They believe their money and power can shield them from any consequences. But they can't hide forever," Benjamin said. "By the way, the University has decided to return Gregory Hale's donations."

Daniel grinned as he leaned forward. "Guess they figured out money that dirty can't even buy decent cafeteria food."

Everyone laughed. "Alice was right all along. She knew what Gregory was doing, and she paid the ultimate price for trying to expose him. But now, Gregory will face justice," I said.

Daniel squeezed my hand, his eyes filled with pride. "Alice would be so proud of you, babe. You never gave up, even when things got tough."

I smiled. "We did it together. All of us."

Eleanor raised a glass of lemonade. "To Alice, may she rest in peace."

We all echoed the toast, lifting our glasses high.

Wyatt leaned in closer. "Emma, there's something else you should know. Detective Brown is under internal investigation."

I looked at him in surprise. "What for?"

"Taking money from Gregory. It seems he was trying to cover up the illegal dumping in exchange for bribes. The investigation is still ongoing, but it looks like justice will be served on that front too."

"I can't believe he would do that."

"Sometimes the truth has more layers than we expect," Wyatt said, taking a sip of his drink. "Here's another piece of good news. Lucas admitted that Gregory ordered him to vandalize your bookstore as a way to intimidate you."

I shook my head. "When I first went to their office, Lucas seemed so professional and polite. It's hard to imagine they would stoop to such malicious actions. I hope they receive the punishment they deserve."

"They will," Daniel reassured me.

I turned to Wyatt and asked, "Have you located the pick-up truck driver who crashed into my car?"

"Yes, we have. He was a hired thug, working for Gregory. He is currently in our custody," Wyatt replied.

"Well, that's a relief," I said.

As I took a sip of iced tea, Eleanor turned to me. "Emma, have you thought about suing Gregory Hale and Lucas Scott?"

I frowned, not quite understanding. "What do you mean?"

"I mean, beyond the criminal charges. There's also the matter of justice for you personally," Eleanor explained. "You could sue them for the pain and suffering they've caused you, the medical bills, and all the expenses that have piled up because of their actions."

Wyatt nodded in agreement. "She's right, Emma. You have every right to seek compensation for the attempted murder of you and Daniel, the vandalization of your bookstore, and the hit-and-run with the pickup truck. Attempted murder isn't just a crime; it's a personal injury too."

Daniel put a comforting hand on my shoulder. "I think Eleanor and Wyatt are right. The compensation could help us with all the expenses we've had to deal with—medical bills, car repairs, everything."

Avery chimed in. "You've been through enough. Taking legal action might be the only way to get justice for you."

The idea of a civil lawsuit had never crossed my mind, but as I looked around at my friends and family, I realized they were right. Gregory and Lucas had turned my life upside down, and there were real costs to that—both emotional and financial.

"I guess I just hadn't thought that far ahead," I said. "I've been so focused on just getting through each day."

Eleanor squeezed my shoulder. "That's understandable, Emma. Now that things have settled a bit, it's time to think about the future. If you want, I can be your lawyer."

"That would be great, Eleanor," I said, taking her hand in mine. "Let's do it. They can't get away with what they've done."

Wyatt smiled. "That's the spirit, Emma."

I scooted over to make room for Benjamin, who had just returned from playing frisbee with Oliver. He cleared his throat and looked at Eleanor before speaking. "I think it's time we made it official."

"Official?" Avery grinned, raising an eyebrow.

"Yes, Avery," Eleanor replied with a smile that lit up her face. "Benjamin and I are together."

"Like a real couple?" Daniel pretended to be surprised, but his eyes showed amusement.

"Exactly."

A chorus of congratulations erupted as we clinked our glasses together in celebration. As the laughter faded into the background, I felt a pull toward the riverbank. I stood up quietly, leaving the chatter behind, and made my way to the water's edge.

The gentle murmur of the river greeted me as I approached, the sound of the water flowing over smooth stones soothing my soul. I looked out over the glistening surface, my heart swelling with memories. This was the place where Alice and I had spent so many summers, swimming and playing in the cool, refreshing water.

I closed my eyes, letting the memories wash over me. I could almost feel the cool water against my skin, and hear the joyful echoes of our laughter as we splashed and raced each other. Alice's face appeared vividly in my mind, her eyes sparkling with mischief and joy. It was as if she were right there beside me, her presence as real and tangible as the river itself.

Tears welled up in my eyes, but I welcomed them. They were tears of love and remembrance, of a bond that transcended time and loss. I opened my eyes and looked out over the river, seeing not just the water but the reflection of all those precious moments we had shared.

At that moment, I felt as if I were back in the river with Alice, swimming freely and happily. The weight of the past months, the pain of losing her, seemed to lift, replaced by a sense of peace. It was as if the river held our memories, preserving them in its gentle current, and reminding me that she was still with me, always.

I took a deep breath, the fresh scent of the water filling my lungs, and whispered, "I miss you, Alice. But I know you're here."